16½ On The Block

A Babygirl Drama

16½ On The Block

A Babygirl Drama

Babygirl Daniels

www.urbanbooks.net

Urban Books
1199 Straight Path
West Babylon, NY 11704

16½ On The Block copyright © 2009 Urban Books, LLC

ISBN- 13: 978-1-60162-183-2
ISBN- 10: 1-60162-183-3

First Printing May 2009
Printed in the United States of America

10 9 8 7 6 5 4 3 2 1

Distributed by Kensington Publishing Corp.
Submit Wholesale Orders to:
Kensington Publishing Corp.
C/O Penguin Group (USA) Inc.
Attention: Order Processing
405 Murray Hill Parkway
East Rutherford, NJ 07073-2316
Phone: 1-800-526-0275
Fax: 1-800-227-9604

Prologue

I can't believe all of what I have gotten myself into this past summer. I'm sitting here looking at these four walls in this small room and wondering how I ended up in a girl's detention home. How in the world did I end up in the State of Michigan system?

Just a few months ago, me and my Cass High School clique were riding in a droptop Lexus and singing Keyshia Cole's new song. We were having the time of our lives. But all that ended way too fast. As I look around this small room, all I can think about is how I would change what I did in the past, if I could.

Oh, I forgot to introduce myself. I'm Latina Smith, the one and only. Whenever I contemplate how much my life changed in such a short time, I get dizzy. As a matter of fact, the room feels like it's spinning out of control right now. Everything seemed to happen so fast.

When I stood in that courtroom and the judge sentenced me to three years in Detroit's Detention Home for Girls, also known as DDHG, I almost fainted. He said that I was a menace to society and in desperate need of rehabilitation.

Whatever! What did that fool know? Obviously he'd been sitting up there on his high and mighty bench too long to know what really goes down in the hood. Me, a menace? I'm just a prisoner of circumstances; circumstances I'd like to think were beyond my control, as far as how things turned out. After all, any chick that has ever been in my shoes would have made pretty much the same choices. Yeah, there are one or two things I would have changed, but in most circumstances, my back was against the wall. My choices were limited—if I even had a choice at all.

No one understands, though, and no one ever will unless they know the entire story of deception, haters, my mistakes, my ups, and my downs. I want every young girl around the country to take heed to the life of Latina Smith, and in the end, know that everything that goes up must come down. I didn't make it up; it's the law of nature.

Remember that everything that seems good isn't always good. I made the big mistake of letting something that seemed good mess up my life. I've heard people talk about that thing called karma all the time, that imaginary force that somehow has the power to come back and bite a person on the butt. Well, take it from me, karma is real, and I am living proof of that. Now I feel as if I owe it to the next chick to keep it real and put my story out there for her to live and learn. So, sit back and pay close attention. I'm about to holla at y'all for a minute and let it be known how one weekend changed my life forever.

See, it all started on the last day of school, heading into the summer of 2009. I was sixteen—well, sixteen and a half . . .

Chapter 1

Latina

It was the last day of school of my tenth grade year at Cass High School, and everyone was anxious about starting their summer break. Kids filed out the doors as if they were animals at the zoo getting let out of a cage. I couldn't blame them, though. I was just as amped as the next person. Those sophomore days were done with, over and gone. I was now finally and officially a junior. Eleventh grade, here I come!

My girls and I were standing around, leaning against Asia's Lexus. Asia was the only one in school driving a $100,000 car. Not even the principal could afford the spaceship that we were sitting on, much less the teachers. It sat on eighteen-inch chrome wheels, and Asia's name was spelled out on the license plate.

Asia was the daughter of a businessman who owned several pizza restaurants in Detroit, and she was spoiled rotten—both her and her half brother. But Asia benefited the most, seeing that her half brother lived with them on the weekends only. Even then, he was usually out, running the streets.

Spoiled or not, that was my girl right there. Asia always wore the flyest gear and rocked the newest purses, coordinated with her shoes, of course. She was the only chick I knew that had a real Gucci purse, not no fake knock-off folks buy at purse parties. And I knew a fake bag when I saw one. Heck, I used to get mine from the bootleg man right off of Seventh Mile. Unlike me, though, Asia could afford the real deal.

She was the envy of most girls at the school. And since I was her girl, that made me one of the most envied too. Heck, if these chicks couldn't be Asia, in their eyes, the next best thing was being next to her as part of the clique. In my own eyes, though, I was more than just the next best thing. Even though I wasn't necessarily cut from the same exact cloth as Asia, I was the real deal too.

Asia and I had been tight since elementary school. Last year, though, she didn't go to Cass. Her dad had forced her to go to a private school, so she and I hadn't hung out as much last year as we had before. As a matter of fact, I rolled with another crew. But when Asia told me that she'd talked her pops into letting her attend Cass, I kicked those chicks to the curb. So this year, it was just Asia and me and one other girl we ended up hanging out with named Gena.

Gena was sooo ghetto, but I loved her. She added an entirely different flavor to our threesome. Even though she was the most petite out of all of us, she had the biggest mouth. While Asia and I always tried to keep it classy with the haters, killing them softy with our attitude and not words, Gena was the total opposite. She would slice a chick up with her tongue, and it wasn't just because she knew Asia and I would have her back if anyone ever tried to step to her. This was just how she got down, not intimidated by numbers or sizes. Catch her rolling with us or catch her flying solo, she was going to speak her mind and handle her business. I'd never had to see her in action, throwing blows or anything. Her bark instilled enough fear in chicks not to want to even test her bite.

Gena always kept long extension braids in her hair; her mom had a beauty shop right off Grand River. Actually, now that I think about it, I'd never seen Gena's real hair. I would sometimes wonder if she was bald-headed under that weave. Well, anyways, even if her hair was fake, in life she always kept it real, no matter what, and I loved her for that.

I met Gena in my freshman year. She was in a couple of my classes. We didn't roll together or anything like that back then, but by the end of our tenth grade year, all three of us were tight like hair weave glue.

As my girls and I bounced our heads to the music that was blaring from Asia's state-of-the-art sound system, we were checking out all the boys and trying to be seen as the sun gleamed down on the car and reflected off the candy-red paint and chrome wheels. The sound of screeching tires erupted, and everyone's focus went to the middle of the parking lot, where Jus was burning rubber on his motorcycle.

Jus is what most would refer to as a bad boy. It was known that he was in the streets and his parents let him do anything he wanted. He had graduated from Cass a couple years ago, but instead of seeking higher education, he sought higher paper in the streets. And like the saying goes—seek and ye shall find—he found it, all right. Maybe that was why his parents let him do whatever, because he took care of his whole family. He pretty much made all the real money up in his house. Jus was what we called a "hood star."

Jus hung out with a boy named Mike. Mike was fine as heck. He had long braids that hung down his back and a baby face, just like I liked it. Picture the singer Omarion, only finer, and that was Mike. I had a little secret crush on him, but I was always too scared to approach him, so he was clueless as to just how much I was digging on him.

"Jus is always trying to show off," Asia snapped as she blocked the sun from her eyes and flopped down into her seat. She had been standing outside her open car door, one foot propped up inside.

"Yeah, but he's cute," Gena said as she hopped in the backseat.

I didn't know what she saw in Jus. He had some big ol' Jay-Z lips and his head was big. I would never talk to him. Besides, one of the girls in the clique I used to hang out with last year had already had him. Sloppy seconds sounded and looked gross in my eyes.

I got into the passenger's side of the car and threw on my shades. "What are we doing tonight, ladies?" I asked as we pulled off.

"I think Mike is throwing a party tonight at the hall on Woodward," Asia said as she maneuvered through the crowded parking lot.

My heart fluttered at the sound of Mike's name, but you know I had to play it cool, like I didn't care.

"I don't know about that. I heard his parties get kind of crazy." I flipped down the visor mirror and checked my hair.

"Girl, please! How you gon' try to front on your girls, of all people?" Asia asked.

I shot her a puzzled look. "What?"

Asia sucked her teeth. "Save it already, Tina. Everybody knows that you got a mad crush on Mike. And with that being said, you trying to be at that party more than anyone. So let's go. It might be fun," Asia said as she flipped down her shade.

"Heck yeah! You know you love you some Mike-Mike," Gena teased.

They were right, and I don't know who I thought I was fooling by acting like I wasn't digging on him. I did think Mike was cute, but it wasn't anybody's business. That's why I chose not to speak on it. And I still wasn't ready to do so. Mike had never really come at me like he was interested, anymore than I had come at him. The last thing I wanted to do was to put my feelings out there, only for them not to be reciprocated. No way was I setting myself up for the okey-doke.

I didn't want to feed into what my girls were saying, so I continued to play the same role I had been playing when it came to my feelings for Mike. "Girl, I don't like Mike. Besides, every girl in school be all over him. I ain't got time to be creating enemies over that big-head boy." I sounded so convincing, I was about to start believing that lie my dang self. "I'll go to the party, though, if y'all trying to go. But I have to ask my mom first," I added.

I skipped a couple songs on the mixed disk that was playing in Asia's system, turned up the music and closed my eyes as I felt the wind blow through my hair. I loved the way it felt riding in a droptop on the highway. We all bounced crazy as the sounds of Soulja Boy's new song bumped.

After we dropped Gena off at her house, not too far from where I lived, my stop was next. Home sweet home . . . the projects. We pulled up to my apartment building, and Asia turned up her nose like she always did. The sight of the crackheads walking around disgusted her, I guess. To her, it was the ghetto, but to me, it was home.

I hopped out of the car and yelled to Asia over the music, "See ya later! Call me in a couple of hours so I can let you know what my moms says about me going to the party." I threw up the peace sign and flipped my book bag over my shoulder.

I watched as Asia sped out of the apartment complex, and then I focused on my building. Who was I kidding? Home or not, I hated it here. It was so raggedy and old. Living in the housing projects was far from luxury, and I couldn't wait until the day when I kissed that all good-bye.

I walked up the stairs that led to my place, pulled out my key and unlocked the door. As soon as I opened it, I heard old-school music coming from the back bedroom. I knew my mother was home . . . and she had company.

A stinky, familiar odor invaded my nostrils, and I knew what was going on in the back. My mother was doing drugs again. I became familiar with the smell of drugs at an early age, and although I hated what she did, that woman in the back bedroom was still my mother.

I had witnessed her downfall because of the drugs, and I vowed to never let a drug enter my body. Not even weed. Although smoking weed was the popular thing to do amongst my peers, I decided not to get into that lifestyle. I had more respect for myself than to fall victim to what many others before me had.

My mom had been battling a crack addiction for as long as I could remember. She spent most of the hours in her day out in the streets, chasing that pipe dream. I basically raised myself, because of her absence. I am an only child, so it had always been just me and my mom. Correction: me, my mom, and the pipe. Regardless, though, of the hand my mother was dealt and how she played it, she was still my mother, and I loved and respected her.

At first I went to my mother's bedroom door, where the music was blaring from. I was going to knock and let her know I was home, but I decided against it. I mean, why bother? Instead, I went to my room to see exactly what I was going to wear to the party later that night. I was sure my mom would let me go. She'd said yes to many things while dazed from her high.

I went through my closet and didn't see anything fly enough to wear for the end-of-the-year bash. On top of that, I didn't see anything fly enough for Mike to see me in. Unlike how it was for Asia, money was tight in our neck of the woods. That meant I didn't have the biggest wardrobe, so I didn't have much to choose from in the first place. But don't get it twisted. In the past, I'd always managed to piece together some one-of-a-kind hookups. And when all else failed, trust and believe ya girl had a Plan B.

I was going to ask Asia if could I wear one of her outfits, but I didn't want anyone to notice that I was rocking my best friend's gear. That would totally ruin my reputation, and with two more years of high school ahead of me, that was not a chance I was willing to take—not even for Mike. Still, I knew I needed something to rock that night. I could not go up into

Mike's party half-stepping. I wanted to be fresh, just in case he happened to notice me. I couldn't ask my mom for any money, because we were broke. The first of the month had come and gone, so I knew my mom's first-of-the-month check was long gone too. Whatever money she might have had before I went to school that morning was now a sticky, yellow substance. I was going to have to get some new gear on my own, but there was one problem—I was dead broke.

I paced my bedroom floor as I thought, *Since when has being broke ever stopped me?*

I called Asia and let her know that I was down with going to the party, but that I didn't have a thing to wear. I asked her to take me to the mall so I could get me something new. Asia always loved an excuse to go shopping, so she was quick to be on her way.

After she picked me up, I gave her directions to Oakland Mall. That was the mall that all the people in my neighborhood shopped at. I had to get an outfit and still have time to go back home and get showered, dressed, and do my hair and makeup, so going to a mall farther out was out of the question for today. Besides, for what was about to go down, I needed to feel at home.

When we pulled up to Oakland Mall, Asia turned

up her nose and smacked her lips. "I don't know how you can shop at this ran-down mall. It's so raggedy-looking," she said as she whipped into a handicap parking spot.

"Well, Miss Big Shot, everyone can't afford to shop at Somerset Mall like you. Everyone doesn't have a rich father, feel me?" I said sarcastically as I opened the door to get out. "Let's go."

When I stepped out of the car, I noticed Asia wasn't moving. I bent down and looked inside only to see her sitting there with her arms crossed, planted in her seat like a stubborn old mule.

"I'm not trying to get seen in this mall. I'll wait outside for you. I don't want to mess up my rep," Asia answered. "Besides, I'm parked in a handicap spot. I need to move the car if I see five-o coming." With that, she turned up her music as if I wasn't even standing there.

I didn't have time to beg her to come in with me, so I left her in the parking lot as I entered the mall. It was probably better that way anyhow. Little Miss Prissy probably would have stood out and drawn more attention than I needed at the time.

The first store I walked into was Macy's. As soon as I walked in, I noticed a tall, dark woman shopping and turned my butt right around and walked back out. See, Macy's think they're slick. They hire fake customers to walk around, pretending to shop, while all they're really doing is keeping an eye on their real customers. But Macy's wasn't fooling me. I knew every store's "pretend" customer that was just waiting to pounce on anyone they spotted trying to shoplift. And me, I wasn't trying to get caught stealing. But, truth be told, I was too good to get caught anyway.

Since Macy's was a no-go, I decided to go over to Fashions Inc. Now, that joint was the hardest store to steal from because they had cameras up around every corner of the store. But the outfit I needed for tonight was crucial, so I would just have to take my chances there. I had to get fly for later that night, and with no cash to my name, I was left with no choice but to engage in every store manager's nightmare: the five-finger discount.

Stealing was a bad habit I'd picked up from my mother while I was growing up. In between the first-of-the-month checks, my mother boosted clothes from stores and sold them half off the ticket price to people in the neighborhood. I started honing in on the craft of boosting quite young, thanks to my mother, and not just because she took me with her on her small heists, but because she used me as part of her scheme.

My mom had me putting clothes in my book bag at

the age of eight. She would make me think we were playing a game called "Don't Let the Security Guard See." I used to have so much fun playing that game at the stores. Mom and I were like the Pink Panther, minus the theme music, creeping up and down the aisles.

I remember one time Mom and I were boosting in a store, and she had just stuffed a black velour jogging suit in my book bag when a female store clerk approached us.

"Excuse me, miss," the clerk said to my mother.

Mom and I nearly jumped out of our skin. I swear her heart and mine were doing a collabo on beats.

Mom put on the best sweet and innocent face she could muster up and replied, "Yes?"

"The store is having a special today." The woman handed Mom a flyer. "If you open up a store credit account with us, you'll get twenty percent off your first purchase. That's five percent more than usual."

"Oh, wow." Mom pretended to be excited as she looked down at the flyer. "I think I just might take you guys up on your offer today. I mean, heck, my money is running so low, every little discount would help."

And, boy, was mom right. Every little discount would help, but as the lady walked off and we walked out of the store loaded with undetected apparel, the one hundred percent discount turned out to be far more appealing than the one the clerk had to offer.

In all honesty, I have to admit that those boosting days with my mom were the best. It was the only memory I had of my mother and I doing something together in those days. But, now, things have changed. She's all about herself, and me, Latina Smith . . . I'm all about me!

Chapter 2

Mike

Life wasn't easy for ya boy. I had two little brothers and one little sister, all under the age of ten. I was the oldest at sixteen, and we all lived with my 67-year-old grandmother, who we called Big Mama. We lived in a three-bedroom house, and it was so cluttered, I could hardly think straight up in that piece.

My grandmother had been taking care of us since I was ten years old, when my mother died from cancer two days before my tenth birthday. Like some of the other kids I grew up around, I never knew my father. Everything had been going good with Big Mama, though—until just recently, when I learned that the wonderful state of Michigan was going to cut off my grandmother's aid for us within the next six months.

I couldn't help but wonder how the government

could be so cold. How did they expect my grandmother to be able to feed us and keep a roof over our
heads without the assistance she'd been counting on
to help her raise us? Without that assistance, she
probably would have never been able to take us in in
the first place. So, of course, deep down inside I feared
that, without that same assistance, she might have to
give us up.

I couldn't see myself allowing that to happen. So I
knew we had to figure out a way to bring more in-
come into the place. Of course, I was the only one of
us kids who was old enough to work. But a sixteen-
year-old can only pull in so many ends—legally, anyway. Keeping it one hundred percent real, I had
thought about going out and hitting these streets to
sell drugs in order to try to help Big Mama out, but I
couldn't run the risk of getting caught and leaving my
siblings and Big Mama to fend for themselves. So, instead, I landed me a gig at the boxing gym around the
corner from our house.

Although it wasn't that far, Big Mama let me use
her car to get back and forth. She said she didn't
want me walking home in the dark. Besides, she never
really drove it anyway. Since I drove it more than her,
everybody just assumed it was my car.

At the gym, I swept the floors and cleaned up the

place three times a week for Mr. Johnson, a former Golden Gloves champion. He was a good guy. He even let me drive his old-school Cutlass some-times—one of the perks of the low-paying job. But I ain't complaining. Every little bit helped.

Another perk was the use of one of Mr. Johnson's other facilities, a building not far from the gym. On occasion he'd rent out the facility to personal train-ers, or boxers who wanted to be trained in private. He'd even rented it out to churches before to hold bingo. Mr. Johnson decided to let me rent it out at a deep discount to throw a big end-of-the-school-year party. All I had to do to repay him for the use of the gym was come in an extra day a week for a couple of months.

With not having to give Mr. Johnson straight-out cash, I had no doubt this party was going to be a come-up. I was going to charge five dollars a person to get into my party. Hopefully, I would make enough that night to help Big Mama with her mortgage this month and maybe even put some of my brothers' and sister's favorite snacks in the fridge as an extra bonus.

I watched as my little brothers and sister came in from school. I had already made them some peanut butter and jelly sandwiches to eat for their after-school snack. It seemed like I had been preparing meals more and more, since Big Mama's arthritis stopped her from moving around a lot.

"'S up, Mike-Mike?" my little sister said as she set her book bag down and hopped in the chair. She was the youngest, at seven years old.

"Hey, big head. Go wash your hands before you eat," I said as I finished putting the paper plates on the table for her and my two brothers, Jake and Blake. They were nine-year-old twins. Bad twins. The doctors said they suffered from attention deficit disorder (ADD), but I think they were just very energetic. It seemed like they moved a hundred miles per hour all the time. I never saw any humans so hyper. They never seemed to slow down.

They ran in and immediately began to pound on the table, trying to do the freshest hip-hop beat they could do.

"Calm down, fellas," I said as I cracked a smile and put their sandwiches on their plates. "Go wash ya hands before you eat."

That's when Angel, my little sister, came from the bathroom with her hands on her hips. "Mike-Mike, the water doesn't work anymore," she complained with a frown on her face.

I took a deep breath and went over to the kitchen sink and turned on the faucet. Nothing came out. The city had finally gotten fed up with all of Big Mama's failed promises to pay and had turned off the water. We had been behind on our payments for three months now, and it caught up with us.

I didn't know what to tell them. I didn't want to let them know we were struggling. I didn't want that on their young minds, so I lied. "The water bandit came and stole all of the water," I told them with a big smile spread across my face.

The kids started laughing, and I was relieved that they'd fallen for it . . . again.

It was just a couple months ago when the television went out right in the middle of our watching a *Diff'rent Strokes* rerun. At first I'd told them that something was wrong with the electric circuit or something; that there was a problem with the fuse box. But then they started demanding that I fix it, and I knew darn well that wasn't where the true problem lay. The three of them had these looks on their faces, urging me to go hurry up and make everything all right. After all, that's what they always expected of their big brother: to make everything all right.

I couldn't let them down. So, after pretending to mess around with the fuse box in the basement, I came back upstairs and gave them the story about the electricity bandit. I compared the electricity bandit to a tooth fairy who runs around stealing teeth.

But then I got stumped when Angel explained to me that the tooth fairy wasn't really a bandit, because at least she left something for what she had taken. Of course, after that, she asked me what the electricity bandit had left for us.

"Candles." Big Mama had saved the day when she came walking out of her bedroom and downstairs to the living room.

"Candles?" my three siblings asked, giving each other puzzled looks.

"What we gon' do with some candles when we ain't even allowed to play with matches?" Angel asked, never the one to leave well enough alone.

"This is what you do." Big Mama walked into the kitchen and pulled out a few candles from a kitchen drawer.

It was only six o'clock in the evening, but the clocks had recently been moved back an hour, so it was dark outside. Big Mama retrieved some small saucers to use as candle holders from a cabinet, then walked over to the gas stove and turned it on its highest temperature until the burners were fire-red. Thank goodness we had a gas stove, and she was able to light the candles by resting the candle wicks on the hot burner until they lit. It probably wasn't the safest thing to do, with all that wax dripping on the burner, but we didn't have any other options. Nobody in the house smoked, so there were no lighters or matches to make the task easier. With the twins being the busybodies they were, Big Mama made sure not to keep any fire-starting materials lying around.

After Big Mama lit the candles, she placed them on the living room table. We all sat around the table while Big Mama led us in some songs she said she used to sing with our mother when she was a little girl. Songs like "There's a Hole in My Bucket," "Mary Mack," and "Found a Peanut." But it was Big Mama teaching us how to sing "Row Your Boat" in harmony that was most fun. I have to admit, for something that could have turned out to be a depressing and frustrating time, Big Mama turned into one of the most memorable times ever.

Because Big Mama had backed me up about the electricity bandit, it now made the story about the water bandit all the more believable.

"Now, get at the table and eat," I ordered my siblings, "so that you guys can start your homework."

I left them at the table and went upstairs where Big Mama's room was. Just as I expected, she was lying in her bed, watching her judge shows. Big Mama loved her some Judge Mathis.

"Hey, Big Mama," I said as I stuck my head in her room.

"Hey, baby. How was school today?" she answered in her raspy voice.

"It was okay. They came and turned off the water today," I said without enthusiasm.

"I know . . . I know, baby." Big Mama struggled a little to sit up in her bed. "Come over here and sit down fo' a minute," she said as she patted the empty spot next to her.

I walked over and took a seat right next to her.

"Times are hard right now, Mike. They gon' be taking away my checks soon, and it's getting too much to take care of all of you already, even with the checks. I have been praying every night, and I know somehow, some way, we're going to be all right. I just need some help, ya know," she said.

Big Mama never really showed weakness, so this was my first time hearing her talking as if she couldn't make everything all right. The same way my younger brothers and sister expected me to always make things better, I expected the same out of Big Mama. But now it seemed as though Big Mama was out of options. I would have to step up big time.

"Big Mama, don't worry about anything. I'm gonna get some money and make sure we're going to be okay." I looked at Big Mama with confidence and put on a fake smile. I knew she was hurting on the inside, and I had to do something about it.

* * *

It was six o'clock in the evening on Friday night, and I only had a couple hours until my party started. It was my goal to set it off proper like, and with the help of my boy, Jus, I had no doubt that it was going to be one of the most talked-about parties since the ones this street cat named Boss used to throw. As a matter of fact, before Flint's finest threw Boss in jail, Jus used to be one of his homeboys. Now it was Jus and I who were tight like the fist on an afro pick.

Jus and I had known each other since we were young, and we'd always been pretty tight. It's just that for a minute there he was extra tight with Boss, and I wasn't into that scene. But now that Boss was out of the picture, we were tight again like the old days.

Jus was the type of dude who lived for the day. He had a crazy personality and a free spirit. He rode his motorcycle like a madman and lived life on the edge. He dealt drugs and always tried to get me to join him in his illegal hustle. But, like I said before, I didn't feel it was worth it. If I ever got caught, it wasn't just about me. My being incarcerated would be affecting other people's lives. My siblings needed me; Big Mama needed me, and I was going to make sure that I was always there for them.

Jus and I were sitting on my porch talking about

the party that was about to go down in a couple of hours. We were just double checking with each other to make sure everything was on point.

"Tonight it's gonna be popping. All the ladies are gonna be all over me. Watch!" Jus yelled as he rubbed his hand over his braids. He had a girl named Summer. To my knowledge, he had never cheated on her, but the male ego in him loved attention from the ladies nonetheless.

I laughed at Jus's arrogance and stared at the ground. I was lost in my own thoughts about how I would come up with the cash for the water to be turned back on.

"So, how much do you make grinding?" I asked my dude—just out of curiosity, of course.

"Man, I get that paper, homey," he said as he pulled out a wad of money.

My eyes lit up when I saw him with all that money. "How much?"

"It all depends. Sometimes I make more in one day than I do in a whole month's work. But sometimes it's slow," Jus said. "And when things get slow, that means some of the other cats on the streets might be going hungry. And them fools might try to do something stupid in order to eat." That's when he pulled out a gun and showed it to me. "But I stay ready for any drama that might come my way."

"Yo, is that real?" I asked as I stared at the iron.

"Yeah, it's real."

Jus must have noticed the way I was admiring the gun, that my hands were a virgin to a cold piece of steel such as that. "Here . . . you can hold it." Jus handed the gun over to me.

I examined it carefully and picked it up and pointed it in the air. It was my first time ever touching a gun.

"You know what? You can hold that for a minute. I have another one," Jus said as he grinned.

"What do you mean? I don't need a gun," I was quick to say as I tried to hand it back to him. If Big Mama ever got wind of me having a gun, let alone bringing one into her house, the next thing to go out would be my lights, because Big Mama sure wouldn't have no problem in knocking them out.

"No, you just hold it for me," Jus insisted as he put his hand up, refusing to take the gun.

Just then I heard the front door creak open behind me, and I knew it was either Big Mama or one of my siblings. I quickly put the gun in my hoodie to get it out of sight.

I wish I had recognized it at that point, but it wouldn't be until later that I realized not giving that gun back to Jus was the biggest mistake of my life.

It wouldn't be the last mistake, either.

Chapter 3

Latina

"Hey, stop!" the guard yelled as he chased me through the mall parking lot.

I had a whole bunch of stolen clothes in my book bag, and I was running for dear life. I was moving as fast as I could to get away from his fat butt, but he was right on my tail. Had he eaten one more donut for breakfast that morning, I think I could have gotten a much better lead on him. Luckily, the lead I had on him was plenty.

I made my way to Asia's car and jumped in. "Drive! Drive!" I ordered her, half out of breath.

Without speaking all the questions written all over her face, Asia sped off quick, fast, and in a hurry. We left the guard in the dust, but only after almost running him over. It was his own fault, though. He tried to play Superman and stop the car by standing in front of it and pressing down on the hood.

"Girl, what happened?" Asia finally asked as she drove out of the parking lot, frequently checking her rearview mirror to make sure we weren't being followed.

I had hoped she'd hold off on the questions for a minute, as I still struggled to catch my breath.

"His fat butt was following me around the store," I replied, breathing heavily. "I think he saw me putting stuff in my book bag on the cameras all along. When I was about to leave, he tried to get close, so I said forget it and took off running."

That wasn't the first time that I used my five-finger discount to get some clothes, and Asia was well aware of my little addiction. So, my story about why the security guard was chasing me was no surprise to her.

I was finally able to catch my breath, and after getting myself together, I pulled out the clothes from my book bag. Although my initial intention when going to the mall was just to get a fly outfit for the party, I had a bad habit of getting greedy and sometimes picking up more than I was supposed to. I had managed to stuff two whole outfits into my book bag this time.

I held up the Baby Phat shirt I had nabbed and examined it.

"That's cute, girl," Asia complimented as she glanced over at the pink shirt.

"Yeah, I know. That's why I got it," I said sarcastically.

With two outfits to choose from, now I was ready to hit the party.

"Now that you're all set," Asia said, "I need to figure out what I'm gonna rock to the party. You know I can't have you outshining me." She winked then asked me to come to her house so that I could help her pick out her outfit.

"No problem," I told her as we detoured from the path to my house and headed for hers.

I loved going to Asia's house. It always reminded me of what I wished I had. They lived in a mini-mansion in Auburn Hills, a suburb just outside of Detroit.

When we pulled into her driveway, I stared at the two-story brick house in awe, daydreaming about living in something so spectacular some day. But how we'd ever afford it was beyond me. Heck, I wish I just knew my father, let alone having one like Asia's, who owned a successful pizza chain and had plenty of loot.

We entered the house, where the white carpet always looked like it was brand-new. It was so bright, it nearly blinded me. They had a cleaning lady that came to the house once a week to keep it on point.

I followed Asia into her room and sat on her bed while she began to search through her nice-sized walk-in closet, which was like a small boutique in itself. Girls like her never had to worry about not having something to wear or how to get it. I guess some people were just more blessed than others.

I wasn't hating on my girl or anything. That was just life. She couldn't help it if her father was about something and mine wasn't crap.

"What do you think about this?" Asia held a black Dior dress up to her body.

Honestly, I thought the dress was whack, but I didn't want to offend my girl, so I lied. And, plus, I didn't want her to look better than me, so it wouldn't hurt any for her to wear that ol' ugly dress.

"Girl, that is too cute," I lied.

"Tina! I know when you're lying!" Asia said with a skeptical look on her face.

I had to admit it, my girl knew me too well. "Okay, okay. That is hideous. Try something else," I admitted with a chuckle that stated *I'm busted*.

Asia continued to look through her closet. We went through at least fifteen outfits, and Asia still wasn't satisfied with one. She finally gave up and closed her closet.

"I'm just going to have to go to the mall and pick out something special for the party like you did. I need to be rocking something new and fly anyway," Asia said as she headed out of her bedroom and down to her living room. I was close on her heels.

"Why didn't you tell me while I was at JCPenney? I would have gotten you something and only charged you half the ticket price," I said. That extra change in my pocket would have done me good.

"I do not wear clothes from JCPenney. No offense or anything, but I just don't get down with that store."

A disgusted look washed across Asia's face. She reminded me of Hilary from *The Fresh Prince of Bel-Air*.

"Just think about it," Asia added arrogantly. "Do you know how many people shop at that store? Too many for me to risk someone having on my same exact outfit. Nine times out of ten they wouldn't freak it like me, but still, I can't take the chance of some chick making me look cheap."

Asia always acted like she was above everyone, but that was just her personality, and she was my girl, so I tolerated it.

I followed her as she made her way to the big painting that hung over their fireplace. As she reached for it, I wondered what in the world she was she doing. How did she go from being desperate about finding an outfit for the party tonight to admiring art?

"What are you doing?" I asked.

"I'm hitting the stash." She took the picture down, revealing a small steel safe that was built into the wall.

"Hitting the stash?" I asked, not knowing what she was talking about.

"Yeah. Any time I need a little extra cash, I just take a little." She said it so nonchalant, as if every girl our age had a safe full of money they could just go hit up whenever they needed some cash.

"Aren't you worried that your father will catch you?" I asked.

Asia proceeded to open the safe, exposing the piles of money inside. I almost choked when I saw how much was in there. Just five minutes ago, I'd almost gone to jail for trying to steal a couple outfits, and this girl had access to enough money to dress everybody at the party. But I wasn't tripping.

"He doesn't even count this. He brings the money from the restaurants in here every night and just dumps it in here," Asia said.

"But how do you know that he doesn't count it at the restaurant before he brings it home?" I asked.

Asia sounded so sure of herself when she replied to my inquiry. "He only counts it when he takes it to the bank Saturday morning."

Asia was telling all of her father's business. And people used to accuse me of having a big mouth and telling everything! Asia had me beat . . . and that is exactly why I never told her anything too important. She couldn't hold water; she would let everyone in Detroit know your business.

As Asia did what she had to do, I went and sat down on the sofa. After Asia took a couple hundred dollars, we left for the mall. This time we went to the one around the corner from her house. The clock was ticking, and we didn't have much time before the party started, so we really needed to put a move on it.

I was really looking forward to partying. . . . Naw, I'm lying. I was looking forward to seeing Mike.

The party was jumping, and the hall was packed. All of Cass High School was there celebrating the end of the school year and the beginning of our summer vacation. You couldn't even tell that the place was a boxing gym. It looked so different. Everyone was going crazy to the Soulja Boy song blaring through the speakers. They were all doing the dance that went along with the song, while I just sat back and watched.

It was dark in the hall, and the only shine was from the strobe lights. I was standing against the wall with my girls, looking at the people on the dance floor. That's when I noticed Mike across the room, standing on the opposite wall. He was surrounded by his boys and seemed like he was looking our way.

I tried to look as good as possible and pretend like I didn't notice him. But how could I not? He was fine. He had neat braids that were so long and thick, and a muscular build that I loved. He was by far the finest boy in school.

I felt Gena nudge me to try to get my attention. "You see Mike over there staring at you?" She sipped her bottled water.

"He's not looking at me," I said as I quickly glanced over there.

"I don't know. It sure looks like he's staring your way to me." Asia just had to add in her two cents. "I'm about to go ask him," she said.

Before I realized what Asia had just said, she was heading over toward Mike and his boys. I turned as red as an apple.

Asia always did crazy stuff like that. One time, when we were all at the mall, there was this dude who worked in the Foot Locker store that kept eyeballing Gena. Unfortunately, he wasn't the most appetizing fry in the combo meal, so Gena tried her best to ignore him. Every time Asia and I nudged her shoulder and informed her that he was still staring her down, she'd get mad. She finally told us that if the boy had looked a little better, she'd at least go out with him, just so she could use his employee discount and buy her some shoes.

Well, the next thing we knew, Gena and I looked up to see Asia over there talking to the guy, pointing at Gena. A few seconds later, Asia came waltzing back over, informing Gena that the guy would be glad to let Gena use his employee discount if she went out with him.

It was a mess. The three of us never laughed so hard in our lives. The very next week, we each got a pair of shoes for almost half off. And Gena got a free meal at O'Charley's.

I had to admit, though, that even if I now knew firsthand how embarrassed Gena must have felt, I watched Asia walk across the room and secretly hoped I'd soon be sharing a meal at O'Charley's with Mike.

I wondered if Asia was really going to talk to him or if she was just trying to get a reaction out of me, a telltale sign of my true feelings for Mike. I glanced over there and saw that she was standing in front of Mike, having a conversation with him. I couldn't believe her!

She talked to him for a couple of minutes before she came back over to us with a big smile on her face. I was ready to curse her out, but she spoke before I could get my words out. "Mike wants to talk to you after the party. He said to meet him on the rooftop afterwards."

I wanted to be mad because Asia went over there and talked to him on my behalf. I didn't want Mike to think I was some punk, or that I was too stuck up to go over there and talk to him myself. But I couldn't help but smile at the result of Asia's efforts. That was the best news of the day. I had wanted to talk to Mike since freshman year.

"Asia, what did you say to that boy?" I had to make sure I wasn't being set up, the same way she'd set Gena up all in the name of a pair of new kicks that she could have afforded at full price ten times over.

"I told him that he needed to stop fronting and come over here and talk to you," she said with a big, cheesy smile.

I playfully punched her in the arm and told her she was wrong, but on the inside, I was glad she, stepped to him for me because, no matter how bold I sometimes believe myself to be, I probably never would have done it myself.

"The party was jumping tonight. What a way to start off our summer," Gena said as we made our way to the parking lot after the party ended.

"Yeah, it was nice," Asia added.

I saw Mike standing right outside the door. He was

surrounded by his friends as he thanked some of his guests for coming to his party.

I don't know how I managed to forget that I was supposed to meet Mike on the rooftop, but I was steady heading to the car right along with my girls.

"Are you going to meet Mike on the roof or what?" Asia asked as we approached her car.

"Oh yeah. That's right," I said.

"Girl, stop playing," Asia stated. "You know you been waiting all night to get with that boy."

"No, for real, I forgot," I told her.

"Yeah, right." She shooed her hand at me like I was a fly. "Anyway, don't be too long. We'll wait for you in the car."

"Oh, that's okay. Y'all don't have to wait for me. I'll see if Mike can just take me home," I told Asia.

That's when I saw Jus and his friend walking toward us. Then there was the sound of police sirens and flashing lights. A swarm of patrol cars sped down the street right past us.

"I wonder who they're after. I wouldn't want to be them," Jus said as he approached us. He threw his arm around Gena, trying to run game. They began to have a personal conversation.

"Are you sure you don't want us to wait?" Asia asked as she hopped on the hood of her car, trying to look cute. "Looks like we gon' be out here a minute anyway." She nodded toward Gena, who was all smiles up in Jus's face.

"Yeah, I can handle myself," I assured her. "I'll call you when I make it home."

"Okay, girl. Have fun," she said devilishly. "But not too much, if you know what I mean."

"See ya, Tina," Gena added as she finished up her conversation with Jus and got in the car.

"See y'all chicks later," I said just before I turned around to see where Mike was at.

I spotted him still standing by the door, talking to Mr. Johnson, the man who owned the place.

Mike just happened to look up while I was standing there gazing at him. I quickly turned my head away so that he didn't think I had been stalking him or nothing like that.

I folded my arms and tapped my foot. I spoke to a couple of people I knew from Cass and then turned my attention back to where Mike had been standing. I saw him by the door, and once again, he saw me. We locked eyes, and then I followed his gaze as he looked up toward the rooftop and then back at me.

He entered the building, and I knew that was my cue.

I smiled and followed him inside, knowing that he

wanted me to come and meet him at that moment. I made my way back inside the door and then up a flight of steps to the rooftop.

When I made it to the top, I saw him standing there, smiling as he stared at me.

"What up, Tina?" he said.

Only my peeps had ever really called me Tina, so the fact that he called me Tina gave me the impression that he just might have been paying a little attention to me after all. "What's up, Mike?"

"Nothing much. Did you enjoy the party?" he asked.

"Yeah, you fixed up Mr. Johnson's place pretty nice. It seemed much bigger tonight for some reason."

"Yeah, Mr. Johnson was cool for letting me throw my party here. It's going to take a few weeks for me to work off the debt, but it was worth it."

"How much does it cost to rent out a place like this?"

"Well, one of my perks for working for him is that I got a discount. But you know how cheap he is. It wasn't much of a discount," he said right before we burst into laughter.

Our laughter faded, and Mike got serious. "Yo, I wanted to holla at you. You know I'm feeling you, right?" he said as he released his charming smile.

I began to blush, not knowing what to say. Then I realized, what better thing to say than the truth?

Heck, I was feeling him too, and I needed him to know. That could make for a much better summer break than playing cat and mouse all summer long.

Before I could open my mouth to answer him, I heard two men yelling at each other from afar. Our eyes shot to the building next door, where we saw two men wearing ski masks on the roof, arguing about something. The buildings were very close, only about two and half feet apart, so we had a pretty clear view of the men, although they were too deep into their argument to notice us.

One man was slim and tall, and the other one was short and fat. Like I said, the men didn't see us; they were too busy cursing one another out. At almost exactly the same time, both Mike and I noticed that the men had guns in their hands. When I saw that, I immediately ducked behind the chimney. Mike followed my lead.

"Did you see that? They've got guns. I wonder what's going on," I whispered as I peeked around the chimney and stared at the two men. One of the men had a duffle bag in his hand, and the other man tried to take it from him.

Mike stood up some and peeked over the top of my head. "I don't know. Seems like they're arguing over that bag." Mike stuck his head out a little more, trying to get a better look.

We both remained silent, almost to the point where we didn't even breathe, so that we could try to hear exactly what was going on.

"Forget that! I'm keeping the money! I don't trust you," the taller man said as he gripped the bag.

"No, I'm keeping the dough!" the other insisted as he reached out for it.

The other man jerked it away before his partner could get a good grip.

"Let's just hide it here until the morning and come back for it. It's too hot for either of us to keep it on us for now."

The men looked around, and Mike and I ducked down, trying not to be seen.

The man with the bag went over to a nearby chimney and stuffed the money in one of its vents. "We'll keep it here and come back for it in the morning."

The shorter man didn't sound like he was down with that. His voice was laced with doubt when he stated, "Naw, man, I don't know about that. Just give me my little cut right here and just go on about our night. You feel me? It ain't like I'm getting much out of the deal anyway."

"Are you dumb? It's too hot right now. The police are all over the place. We need to dump it here."

"I guess that's cool. But don't try any funny stuff. We'll meet back up here tomorrow first thing."

"Okay."

They both took off their masks and tossed them over to our building. They landed right by us. My heart began beating fast. I was scared that the men would see us hiding, but I guess they didn't, because they exited the roof.

"Did you see that?" Mike asked as he slowly rose up.

"Yeah. This is some crazy stuff," I answered.

Silence rested between us momentarily as we looked over at the other building's chimney. We then looked back at one another as if we'd both been thinking the same thing.

"We should go and see how much is over there," Mike said.

"Yeah, but how are we going to get inside that building?"

Mike thought momentarily. "There must be a fire escape. Isn't that how dudes just did it?" Mike walked over near the edge of the rooftop and looked toward the building where the duffle bag was hidden. "Matter of fact, it's not that far of a jump." He examined the distance. "Two feet, three feet tops, from here to there."

I visually measured the distance myself, and Mike was right; it didn't seem too far to jump. I looked up at Mike, and that's when I saw the familiar look of greed in his eyes. It was a trait of every ghetto child. No matter who the daddy was, we all inherited those eyes.

For a minute, I was skeptical about getting involved, but that duffle bag seemed full, and I was in desperate need of money—another trait of the ghetto child.

I thought for a moment before replying, "Let's wait a few minutes just to make sure they're gone first, and then we'll go over."

The look on Mike's face was unforgettable. He looked at me like I was the Bonnie to his Clyde. He nodded his head in agreement, and after a couple minutes, we headed over.

Chapter 4

Latina

What I saw made me almost want to scream. As Mike fingered through the hundred-dollar bills, I got a rush. I had never seen so much money in my life. Not even the stash in Asia's safe had made my jaw drop to the ground like all this green in front of me.

Mike had jumped first over to the rooftop, and I had followed. The jump was easy. I simply did as Mike instructed and didn't look down.

"Oh my God. I can't believe this," I said, putting my hand over my mouth in disbelief. Mike's mouth was dropped to the ground.

"This is a whole bunch of money. Let's take it," Mike said as he zipped up the bag and prepared to take it with him no matter what my reply was.

But I was no fool. Who in their right mind could leave that much money and sleep well knowing it was there? Obviously those two masked men could, but surely not me and Mike.

I nodded my head in agreement, and then Mike made sure he got a good grip on the bag, and we jumped back over to Mr. Johnson's building rooftop the same way we had come over. We hurried out of the building and ran out to the parking lot and over to Mike's car.

We rode in silence, neither of us knowing what to say. The only time I spoke was to tell Mike to go left or to go right in order to get to my place. As we pulled up to my apartment building, I looked over at Mike, wondering what we were going to do with all the money.

He pulled in front of my building and put his car in park. He took a deep breath and looked over at me, then grabbed the duffle bag from the back seat and placed it on his lap.

"This is a lot of money."

"Yeah, it is. What are we going to do with it?" I asked.

"What do you mean? We're going to keep it. Spend it. Pay some bills. But I just have to figure out how. I mean, this is a lot of dough to just be spending, and I know the two men are gonna be looking for whoever has this bag as soon as they go up there and find that the chimney's empty." Mike paused for a minute while he thought, and then as if all of his thinking was in vain, he said, "I'll figure out something."

"You're going to have to, because we can't just start spending it freely. The way those two men were acting up on that roof, you know they took it from somebody, and that only means one thing—those two won't be the only ones looking for this cash."

"You're right," Mike said, then once again, he began to look as though he was deep in thought. "Our first date was crazy, right?" He looked over at me with a smile on his face.

His smile relaxed me, took my mind off of our current situation for a minute. "Yeah, I guess you can say that." I smiled back.

I didn't know what to do next. My mind went back to the big bag full of cash in front of us that neither one of us knew what to do with. Now I understood why those two men were arguing on the rooftop like they were. What was one supposed to do with all of this stolen money?

"Okay, look, you keep it until the morning, and then we'll decide what to do with it next. I can't take it home without risking the chance of my grandmother asking too many questions. She knows stuff that I don't even know how she knows about it."

I didn't really have a problem with that. My mom

never had her nose in my affairs. She was always too busy worrying about her next hit. Of course, I would be taking the risk that she would find the money, but I didn't have to worry about her asking any questions. She'd simply smoke it all up, and Mike and I would be no better off than had we left it up there on the rooftop.

"Okay," I agreed as I inhaled deeply and grabbed the bag. I opened the car door and started to step out.

Mike grabbed my hand, and I looked back at him.

"Don't tell anyone about this, and keep it in a safe place, Tina," he instructed as he looked directly in my eyes.

I nodded my head in agreement and headed to my apartment with the money.

When I entered the apartment, it was quiet, and all the lights were off. I knew my mother was asleep because I heard the sound of her snoring coming from the back room. I was glad she was knocked out so that she wouldn't be all in my face when I came in. She never really questioned me when I came in anyway, so I didn't expect a problem from her, but I was still relieved.

I went to my room, turned on the lights, and then locked the door. I emptied the entire contents of the bag onto my bed and viewed all of the cash that lay sprawled out. "Oh my goodness!" I was trying my best not to be loud, but a sistah was paid!

I put the money back in the bag and stepped outside of my room. There was a square on the ceiling in the hallway, right where the attic was. I pulled the string down to release its mini steps and then went up and stuffed the money up there. I knew it would be a good spot to hide it because no one ever went in our attic. There were only old Christmas ornaments up there from years back. Ever since my mom had gotten bad on the drugs, we never had Christmas anymore, so I knew the money would be safe.

I made sure the bag was in place and then closed the attic. I returned to my room and flopped down on my bed. I was sleepy, but the excitement of having all that money kept me anxious and awake. I could get anything I wanted now with all that cash. I could get anything I wanted without having to steal it. But what excited me most was that I could move me and my mother out of the projects for good and never look back. I was in heaven . . . well, at least I thought I was, but where there is a heaven, there is a hell. Hell would come in the morning.

Chapter 5

Luke and Goon

Luke and Goon hid behind the dumpster, trying to avoid being seen by the police vehicles that crept past the alley. They had just hidden the money from an after-hours bank robbery. Luke tried to duck down as far as he could, but he was so tall that his head slightly showed over the dumpster. Goon, who was shaped like a pear, was breathing heavily and ready for his next meal.

"Did you brush your teeth today, man? Whew! It smells like your mouth just farted," Luke said as he covered up his nose.

Goon smacked his lips in embarrassment. "I forgot, man. Why are you always in my business anyway?" Goon asked, getting loud.

"Shhh! The police car just stopped right in front of the alley," Luke whispered. He put his finger over his lips, signaling Goon to quiet down. That's when he looked up and saw a young boy and girl leaping from one rooftop to another . . . to the same rooftop where they had stashed their money. "What the—?" Luke kept his eyes up toward the rooftop.

It wasn't but a minute later when he saw them jumping back to the rooftop from which they'd originally come. And if his eyes weren't deceiving him, the boy had their duffle bag in his hand.

"Man, he got our bag," Luke whispered in disbelief. He stared helplessly. They couldn't go after them, because the cop was parked on the opposite end of the alley and would see them if they went into plain sight.

Goon jumped up from his crouched position in attempt to go after their money, but Luke quickly yanked him back down.

"Let 'em go."

"Man, what do you mean, let 'em go? That's our money," Goon spat.

"I've seen him before. He works for Mr. Johnson at the gym right there, and he lives right by the projects by my aunt. I know exactly where he lives too. Don't worry about it. We'll catch up with that little punk,"

Goon said through his clenched teeth. "I'm sure him and his little girlfriend will take good care of our money until morning."

Luke and Goon had to wait until the cop pulled off before they could leave. It was going to be a long night. The entire Detroit police department was looking for two men that fit their description. They could only watch as the young boy and girl exited the building. Then they heard a car start and pull away—with all their money—and they couldn't do anything about it. Not yet anyway.

Chapter 6
Latina

The sound of rocks tapping my window right by my bed awoke me. I opened my eyes and sat up, wondering what the noise was. I wiped the sleep out of my eyes and opened up my window. I saw Mike standing one story down, about to throw another pebble.

"Boy, is you crazy?" I yelled as I looked down at him.

"Sorry. I didn't know how to get your attention. I didn't want to just come knocking on the door," he said with a slight grin.

"What you doing? Checkin' up on me to see if I was trying to get away with all the loot or something?" I joked. "Did you expect to show up and find me and my moms loading a U-Haul truck, about to get ghost?"

Mike shook his head and smiled.

"Hold on, boy. I'll be down in a second," I said, smiling back.

I closed my window and walked over to my dresser and opened a drawer so that I could put something on. I rubbed the back of my neck gently to try to loosen it up. I had been twisting and turning all night, thinking about all the cash we had come up on.

I slipped on a tee-shirt and some sweat pants and headed down to talk to Mike. I knew he was itching to figure out what we would do with the money. He probably had been tossing and turning all night, too, which was why he was now waking me up out of my uncomfortable, restless sleep.

I entered the living room and heard the television blaring. I called for my mom, but no one answered. I went to her room and opened the door, but it was empty.

"Where did she go so early?" I asked myself as I frowned up.

I walked over to the television to at least turn it down, but then something on the screen caught my attention. I saw a special bulletin alert. I listened closely when I heard something about some stolen money.

"This is Alicia Fields reporting," the female news reporter said. *"Last night, the First National Bank on Woodward was broken into. Authorities say that two*

*masked men managed to escape with thirty thousand
dollars in cash. The robbers disabled the alarm system and managed to escape undetected. It wasn't
until the hired security company made a random
visit to the bank that it was discovered to have been
broken in to. The only evidence of the robbery is this
surveillance footage that captured the entire thing."*

I could not believe what I was seeing. The two
masked men on the surveillance video were the same
men we saw hiding the money. That meant that the
money in my attic came from a bank robbery.

I turned off the television and then ran down the
stairs to tell Mike what I had just seen. On my way
down, I was having second thoughts about keeping
that money. Honestly, I wanted to keep the money,
but I did not want to be involved in a bank robbery.
What if the bills were marked or something? The last
thing I wanted to do was go down for a bank robbery
that I had nothing to do with. On the other hand, I
was no bank robber and I knew it. So to justify keeping the money, I had to remind myself that it wasn't a
crime to find money and not turn it in, was it?

When I reached the bottom steps, I saw Mike waiting for me. I guess he saw the look in my eyes, because his smile turned into a frown.

I said, "I saw some crazy stuff on the news just
now. The money—"

Mike cut me off by putting his finger over my lips. "Shhh!" he whispered.

I was so worried, I did not realize that I was nearly yelling. "Sorry," I apologized and then regained my composure. "I just saw the two men that were on the roof on TV just a minute ago. They robbed the bank on Woodward," I said with a shaky voice, talking ninety miles per hour. At least I wasn't yelling this time though.

"I know. I saw it this morning too." Mike looked around to make sure no one was listening in on our conversation, and then he pulled me over to a nearby bench. "We're in the perfect situation. The cops are looking for two grown men. We have the cash and no connection to the robbers. We're basically scot-free," he said confidently.

"What are you talking about?" I asked as I frowned up, thinking he was talking crazy. While what I'd just seen on television scared me to death and had me contemplating turning in the money, this fool was acting like we'd hit the lottery and had won the money legitimately.

"You don't get it? We can keep the money with no worries," he said confidently as he checked around again.

For some reason, I just sat there staring at him and noticing how fine he was. My nostrils took in that good-smelling cologne he had on. He smelled so good. He looked so good.

"Where's the dough?" he asked, snapping me out of my trance.

"It's upstairs." I pointed upward, toward my apartment.

"Go get it. Let's split it up in my car," he said as he stood up and hit the alarm on his Grand Prix. "The news said it's about thirty G's. That's fifteen G's each." He rubbed his hands together in anticipation.

I nodded and headed upstairs to get the bag. I ran up and into the house excited about counting the cash.

Mike's theory about the money had made me feel one hundred percent better, so my mind was made up. I definitely didn't want to turn in the stolen money. I wanted to spend it!

Mike was right. That news reporter said it was nearly thirty thousand dollars, and that meant only one thing—I was rich! I rushed into my apartment and through the living room into the hallway. I reached up to pull down the attic door. What I saw next made my heart drop. The attic door was slightly open. I knew for sure that the night before I had closed it all the way shut. I immediately got worried.

"No. Please, no," I whispered as I yanked down the string and opened the door completely. I climbed up and stuck half of my body in the attic, and I saw nothing but Christmas ornaments. The duffle bag was gone! The money was gone!

I had to take several deep breaths in order to slow down my breathing. I thought I was going to hyperventilate and have to call 9-1-1.

Once I got my breathing under control, I climbed down out of the attic and leaned against the hallway wall in disbelief.

"I can't believe this!" I yelled as I shook my head from side to side. That's when I heard my mother come in the door.

"Mom!" I yelled. I knew she had something to do with the missing duffle bag. I didn't want to believe she had gotten a hold of the money, but I knew better. "Where is it?" I asked her with a ray of hope. I don't care how much she loved crack; there was no way she could have smoked up thirty thousand dollars worth already.

"Where is what, baby?" she asked with a glazed look in her eyes.

I knew she had been doing drugs. I could tell whenever she was high. It hurt my heart every time I saw my mom like that, but right now, my focus was recovering that duffle bag, hopefully with the money still in it.

"The bag! You know what I'm talking about," I

yelled. I had never disrespected my mother before by yelling at her, and the look on her shocked face confirmed it.

"Baby, I don't know what you're talking about. Are you okay?"

"I had a bag with my belongings in there,"—I pointed to the attic—"and now it's gone." I swear, just saying those words, I wanted to bust out crying. But I maintained my composure.

"I didn't touch your things," she said as she went and sat lazily on the couch.

I looked at my mother, and I could tell she wasn't lying. I knew her like the back of my hand, so I could always tell when she was telling the truth or not. This time, she was truthful.

"Well, who else was here?" I asked as I began to anxiously pace the room.

"Ray spent the night with me last night," she said, almost nodding off in the middle of her sentence.

"Where is he?" I exclaimed.

"He rushed off this morning in a hurry. He left about seven," Mom said, barely able to keep her eyes open at this point.

I knew right then and there who had the cash. Ray was a known thief and crackhead. He would steal your dreams if he could. He was that bad of a thief. But right now, Ray wasn't there to take the blame, so

I quickly turned to the only other person there who could take responsibility for my loss.

"Why did you let him in here? You know he's a thief!" I screamed.

My mother didn't even reply to my ranting and raving. She was well into the snoring stages by now. I wanted to shake her awake and tell her how serious this matter was, but I didn't want to tell her exactly what it was that Ray had stolen.

I knew that yelling and carrying on wouldn't get the money back. Mike and I were going to have to find Ray ourselves before he spent all of the money.

Chapter 7

Luke and Goon

Luke snatched off his jacket as he climbed the stairs to his apartment building. Goon was a couple steps behind him, and he could hear him breathing hard. He looked at his watch and saw that it was almost seven o'clock in the morning. The stupid cop had spent the remainder of his shift blocking that alley and scoping out the neighborhood. Luke and Goon were heated that they had to spend the night in a nasty alley behind a stinking dumpster.

Luke got to his door and slowly put the key in. He didn't want to wake his son and wife.

Goon had heavy feet, so he came in stomping loudly. Luke turned around and smacked Goon in the back of the head and whispered, "Be quiet, man! Li'l Luke is in there 'sleep!" Luke nodded his head toward his young son's bedroom.

"Sorry, Luke," Goon apologized as he walked on his tippy toes.

If it weren't for the fact that Goon was Luke's brother, Luke would not have let him come stay at his spot. But Goon was fresh out of jail and didn't really have anywhere else to lay his head.

"You can crash right there on the couch, bro. I'll see you in the morning," Luke said just before he disappeared into the back room.

Goon flopped on the couch, and within two minutes, he was knocked out cold.

Luke walked into his son's room and saw him sleeping peacefully in his bed. Li'l Luke was only four years old and was disabled. He was born terribly bow-legged and was never able to walk properly. It hurt Luke's heart every time he saw his son have to sit while the other kids played. The doctor said Li'l Luke would be able to walk if he got a surgery to repair his badly bowed legs, but it would cost major paper. Luke didn't have insurance, so he had the burden of getting the money for the surgery himself.

Luke couldn't get a decent-paying job with benefits because no business owner in Detroit wanted to hire an ex-con. That's why the money from the bank robbery was so important to him—and he couldn't believe that he had been forced to watch it slip away from him. He had to get that money back. A normal life for his son depended on it.

He looked down at his son again then leaned over and kissed him on the forehead. "I love you, Li'l Luke," he whispered. "I'm gonna do everything possible to make sure that one day you'll walk."

Luke went into his bedroom and got into bed with his wife, who, unbeknownst to him, was already awake.

"Luke, what happened, baby? Where were you?" she asked in more of a concerned tone than a nagging one. "Did you have any luck getting a job yesterday? I figured you must have gotten picked to do some day labor or something."

It wasn't out of the ordinary for Luke to go to one of those hiring sites where contractors came in looking for laborers to finish up construction jobs. A couple times before, he'd had to spend some all-nighters working on projects so that his family could eat.

"No, I didn't get a permanent job or anything. But, baby, I got the money for Li'l Luke's surgery," Luke said.

His wife sat up with a frown on her face. "Luke, if you didn't get a job, then how did you get the money?" She gave him a suspicious look. "You and that brother of yours aren't getting into anything illegal, are you?"

"No, of course not. I'm not going back to jail!" Luke said in an adamant tone. "I just have some money coming my way, that's all." He thought up a quick lie. "An old friend repaid a debt to me."

"Luke, the surgery and the physical therapy is going to cost over twenty-five thousand dollars, baby. Who in the heck owed you that kind of money?"

"Don't worry. I got it," Luke said as he turned over and thought about how badly he needed all the money, and how he was going to do anything within his power to get it back so that his son could walk. Anything!

Chapter 8
Latina

"**Y**ou've got to be kidding me. It's gone? Where is this guy Ray at?" Mike asked as he buried his face into his steering wheel.

I had just broken the news to him about the missing duffle bag, and he began to panic. I felt so bad about being so dumb. I guess the only thing that made me feel better about the situation was that not once did Mike even look at me sideways, like I might have been lying and was just trying to keep all the money for myself.

"Where?" Mike asked. "Where does Ray stay at?"

Although Mike was in panic mode, I tried to remain calm and think.

"Okay, he lives in the projects, so it shouldn't be too hard to find him. He has a bad drug problem, so we should look at all the drug spots," I said, knowing that I had made a big mistake by not keeping the bag closer to me. So many woulda, coulda, shouldas ran through my head. I shoulda put it here, if I woulda put it there, if only I coulda . . . but that type of thinking wasn't going to get us anywhere.

I could tell Mike was very disappointed. He looked at me with a lost expression. I couldn't help but to feel terrible. My carelessness had just cost us a lot of money.

"Well, sitting here ain't gon' get us nowhere." Mike sighed. "I guess we better—"

Just as Mike was about to finish his sentence, there was a thud from the back doors of his car opening. Before either of us could turn our heads around, two men came from each side of the car and jumped into the backseat.

They grabbed us both from behind. I began to scream until the man who had grabbed me put his hand over my mouth to stop my cries. I tried my best to look over and see what was going on with Mike. That's when I saw the man behind Mike put a knife to his neck.

"Where is my money?" the man yelled at Mike. He bore this crazed look in his eyes.

Mike began to sweat bullets, and I could see he didn't know what to tell the man.

"I don't know what you're talking about," Mike lied.

The man let out a sinister chuckle. "Oh, you think it's a game, huh?" The man punched Mike in the back of the head. "You want to play stupid, huh?" He punched Mike again.

I watched as Mike's head jerked from the impact of each blow. Mike held the back of his head in agony as I watched helplessly.

"We saw you leave the building," the man said into Mike's ear. "You and your little girlfriend here got our dough, and don't try to deny it. We watched you both like y'all was some ghetto Spiderman or something, jumping from building to building. But I ain't mad. Thirty G's is worth the fall—only, you didn't fall."

I could tell the man must have pressed the knife harder against Mike's neck, because he began to tense up.

"You just got away before we could catch up to you," the man told him. "You thought we wouldn't find you, but I knew exactly where to find your little punk self. Only problem was, I didn't know whether you or your girl had stashed the money, so I needed to make sure I killed two birds with one stone and got y'all together. Good lookin' out on leading us straight to ya girl this morning." Once again, he let out a sinister laugh. "Now, where is the money?" he demanded to know.

I wanted to say something, but what was I supposed to say? Mike really didn't know where the
money was, and neither did I. We knew who had it,
but that was about it. I knew Ray stayed in the projects, but I didn't know exactly where. It wasn't like
Mike and I could just take these fools straight to
Ray's doorstep or anything. For all I knew, Ray was
long gone out of town, spending the money by now.

I saw the man that was behind Mike cock back his
hand, preparing to strike Mike again. I couldn't bear
it any longer. That's when I started squirming and trying to talk with the other man's hand still over my
mouth.

"Let her say what she's got to say, man," the dude
behind Mike said to his partner. "Perhaps she's a lot
smarter than her boyfriend and is ready to talk."

The man removed his hand from my mouth. "And
you better not scream," he warned me.

I immediately spoke. "The money is gone!" Tears
began to form in my eyes. I was so scared.

Mike shot me a look of disappointment for not
backing up his initial claim. He didn't want me to
admit that we had the money in the first place, but it
was obvious that they already knew. The one man
had described our actions like he'd watched us up on
an IMAX screen.

Upon my confession, the attention of both men focused on me. The one who had been harassing Mike turned his interrogation to me. "What do you mean, the money's gone?"

I took a deep swallow and looked over at Mike. Although his eyes were begging me not to say anything else, I went against his nonverbal request and spoke anyway. "It's gone. We don't have it," I stammered. "I mean, we had it. I had it. I hid it in my house, but then some crackhead friend of my mom's stole it from my attic. That's where I had hid it." I was singing like a trained hummingbird as tears fell rapidly from my eyes.

The man who had the knife on Mike began cursing and hitting the back of the seat in frustration. The tension grew as I wondered what they were going to do with us. That's when I felt a hand go over my mouth tightly. I could smell the stink breath of the man behind me.

"Well, you better find homeboy and come up with my cash," the one who had been doing all the talking said.

His partner decided to chime in with a threat of his own. "You two got twenty-four hours to have the dough, or you're both dead," he said in my ear.

The other man grabbed Mike around the neck and whispered in his ear loud enough for me to hear him. "Don't think you can just run off, li'l dude. We've been following you all morning, thinking you were going to lead us to where you put the cash. So we know where you and your family live. There is no running. And if you notify the police"—The man used the knife to make a cutthroat gesture on his own neck. "Twenty-four hours! We want you to meet us right back here, and if you don't have our money, you can kiss Christmas goodbye."

Chapter 9
Latina

Mike and I were on the steps of the big white house on the corner of 7 Mile. Everyone knew it was the go-to drug house and that every user from our projects usually went there. I was skeptical about walking in at first, but we needed to find Ray. It wasn't just about getting the money back so that we could spend it. It was now a matter of life and death— the life and death of both Mike and me and our families.

If anything happened to Mike and his family or my mom, I didn't know what I'd do. I felt responsible for being so careless with the money, and I was going to try my hardest to find Ray's ol' crackhead butt.

"You ready?" Mike asked as he walked up to the porch ahead of me.

There were men and women standing outside the house like vultures around road kill. The looks in their eyes were that of pain and lost souls. The foul body odor hit me, and I turned up my nose in disgust.

"Let's hurry up and get out of here," I added as we walked into the drug house.

People were scattered around the room, using their preferred drugs. The room was dim and damp. The smoke in the air made it feel like we were walking into a dream, or better yet, a nightmare. I couldn't help but think that this was probably where my mother had laid her head on more occasions than enough. I mean, in the past, I had the pleasure of only imagining what it was like for my mother out here on the drug scene. But now, unfortunately, the pleasure was all mine, right here in the flesh. I don't know if I was more saddened or sickened by what I was experiencing.

I had described to Mike what Ray looked like on the way over to this place, so both of us scanned every corner of the room as we made our way through.

"Do you see him?" Mike whispered as he leaned close to me.

"No, he's not in here. But I'm sure someone in here knows where he's at. A crackhead carrying around a bag full of money isn't hard to notice." I looked around to double-check that he wasn't in there.

Mike reached into his pocket and pulled out a crumpled ten-dollar bill and held it up in the air. "I got ten dollars for whoever can tell me where Ray is at," he said loudly.

"Ray who?" somebody shot back.

"Heck, give me the money and I will personally take you to his house," another fiend offered.

That was even better, as far as I was concerned. Mike and I looked at each other and smiled, knowing we were making progress. It seemed as though the hunt for Ray was going to be easy. I hoped getting that money from him would be just as easy, but something told me it wouldn't be.

As we walked up to the small brick house, the man who had brought us there displayed his toothless smile and held his hand out. "Okay, you said if I showed you where Ray lived, you would give me ten bucks." He pointed to the house. "Well, here it is. Ray's mother left him this old raggedy house, and he's been here ever since."

Mike gave him the money and told him to get lost. The fiend's eyes lit up like he had just won the lottery. Just as fast as Mike handed him the money, he was gone.

Mike looked at me and said, "I hope he's in there."

"What if ol' dude was lying? What if Ray really

doesn't live here?" I said with doubt. "Shouldn't we have checked first before giving him the money?"

"I'm sure he lives here. I mean, who would go through all of that trouble for a lousy ten bucks?"

"Duh . . . a crackhead," I said, putting my hands on my hips.

Mike rolled his eyes with a chuckle. "Come on, girl. Let's go."

We walked up to the door. The cracked concrete porch was filthy, and there were empty beer bottles all over. The odor made me gag. It smelled like who-ever had consumed all the beer had turned around and released it right back out on the porch.

I held my nose as Mike opened up the screen door, prepared to knock. His hand froze midair when he noticed that the front door was already cracked open.

He looked back at me and whispered, "It's open. Let's go in."

It was probably better if we didn't knock, giving Ray a heads-up to hide the money or make up a lie, so I nodded my head in agreement and we slowly crept in. The place was trashed. It didn't look or smell any better than the front porch. Rotting food and empty bottles of liquor were scattered all over. The living room's table was full of needles for drug use, and crack pipes.

We could hear the television in the back of the one-story house and instantly knew someone was there. Mike pointed, signaling that we should go back there. I put my hand over my nose, and we stepped over the items on the cluttered floor, heading for the back room.

We crept up on a man sitting in a La-Z-Boy chair. I knew it was Ray because of his old, dusty fro. Yuck! I had no idea how my mom could stand the sight of him.

His back was turned toward us, so he didn't even see us coming. Mike crept up behind him and grabbed him, but he wasn't prepared for what he saw. Ray had a syringe stuck in his arm, and his eyes were open . . . dead open.

"Oh, shoot!" Mike yelled as Ray's limp body fell over onto the floor.

"Oh my God!" I yelled as my knees got weak. I had never seen a dead body before.

"He's dead," Mike said in disbelief as he stepped away from the body. It was obvious that Ray had overdosed on the drugs he'd shot up in his veins and had died while getting high.

"Let's get out of here," I muttered as I backed out of the room in total shock. This entire scene was getting to be too much for me. I never saw anything like this coming.

"We can't leave without the money, Tina," Mike said, reminding me why we'd come in the first place.

Mike's eyes began to search the room. He rummaged through the things in the room with total disregard to the dead body in the middle of the floor.

I couldn't tolerate being in the room with a dead body any longer, so I went to look through the rest of the house. After rummaging through that pig sty, I didn't see any sign of the money.

I went back in the bedroom and saw Mike going through Ray's pockets. He pulled out a wad of money and held it up to show me.

"Well, we know he did have the money." Mike shook his head, looking defeated. "I bet whoever he was . . . whoever he was getting high with . . . probably took the money," he said in disappointment.

We were back to square one, but now we had no idea what steps to take next. How in the world were we going to find the money now? Finding Ray's get-high buddy would have been like trying to find a needle in a haystack. Then something suddenly dawned on me. What if my moms had been Ray's get-high buddy? What if she really knew exactly what I was talking about but was just playing stupid?

Even though my mom had chosen drugs over me on numerous occasions, I just couldn't allow myself to believe that she would lie to me about something like this. I wouldn't allow myself to believe that, quickly erasing the thought from my head.

Mike and I walked into the living room, still searching around, as if the money was just going to appear out of nowhere. An expression of sorrow emerged on Mike's face. He looked like he was about to cry. He tried to hide it, but I saw right through him.

"I can't let my family get hurt." Mike shook his head. "Those guys were animals. We don't have any money for them, and I don't know what to do," he said, holding his head down.

Once again, I felt like it was all my fault. I was the one who put the money in the attic, knowing my mother kept traffic in and out of the house. But I never thought in a million years anyone would go in that attic, and I couldn't imagine what made Ray look in it.

Since this was my fault, I had to be the one to think of something, and quick. Just then, a sudden thought came to mind, and a smile crept across my face.

I went over and hugged Mike, who had a look of confusion on his face. I told him, "I have a plan." I knew once I shared it with him, his look of confusion would turn to a smile.

Chapter 10

Latina

I couldn't believe what I was getting ready to do. I felt so bad.

As we sat in Mike's car, two houses down from Asia's house, I watched as Mike nervously tapped his steering wheel.

"Are you sure that he keeps money in the safe?" he asked me.

"Yeah, I saw Asia take some out yesterday. He doesn't even have a lock on it. It's just hidden behind a painting in the living room."

"And you're sure that he isn't home?"

"He doesn't make it home until a little after nine. It's only three now, so I know Asia is in there by herself."

"Okay, call her and tell her to meet you some-where. Make it sound like an emergency, so she can rush out. Then I'll break into the house and take the money," he said.

"How do you know how to break into a house, Mike?" I asked out of curiosity. Even though Mike and Jus were cool, I knew they weren't cut from the same cloth. Mike might have been from the streets, but he wasn't street. He just never came across to me as being built to do this type of thing.

"I am not as innocent as I look," Mike assured me as he reached into his backseat and pulled out a gun.

I jumped in terror. Once again, the last person I ever expected to be packing was Mike.

"Boy! Where did you get that thing from?" I yelled.

"Never mind that. Just be glad that I do have one, in case something unexpected jumps off."

"What do you mean, unexpected?" I asked out of concern. It was bad enough that I was aiding in the break-in of my homegirl's house. I didn't want her to get shot up in the process. That was definitely not part of the plan.

"I ain't talking about shooting nobody, girl," Mike told me. "Do I look like a killer to you?"

"No," I was quick to say. "You don't look like someone who breaks into houses, either, but you're doing that."

"Look, I'm not bringing it to shoot anybody. I'm just bringing it in case I need to scare her or something. You feel me? Dang." Mike shook his head.

I watched how he held the gun like an amateur. I could tell he didn't know what he was doing. I didn't understand what the gun was for anyway. You scare a person by shooting a gun, not just showing it to them. That was gun rule number one: Don't pull it out unless you plan on using it.

"Mike, I don't think the gun is a good idea. You could really hurt somebody with that," I pleaded with him. After watching him carelessly hold that gun, I felt as though he was in more danger than Asia was. He was liable to blow his own brains out.

"Just call her, Tina," he ordered, disregarding what I had just said.

I picked up my cell phone and dialed Asia's number. Moments later, she picked up the phone.

"Hey, Asia. I need your help," I said, pretending to be out of breath.

"Tina, is everything okay, girl?"

Asia sounded truly concerned. It almost made me want to reconsider the plan. Maybe I could just let her know about the mess Mike and I were in and ask her if we could have the money.

But who was I kidding? I couldn't even ask the girl to borrow money for an outfit, let alone thirty thousand dollars. Nope. We had to stick with the plan.

"Yeah, um . . . I got two Oakland Mall security guards chasing me, and I need you to come and get me," I told her.

"Girl, you crazy. You're going to get caught one of these days. How did you get out there in the first place?"

"I caught the bus. But never mind all that. I need a ride home."

"Well, take the bus back home, girl. *Flavor of Love* is on, and I'm not trying to miss it."

I couldn't believe this chick. Here I could have really been in a life-and-death situation, and this girl was worried about Flavor Flav. Now I didn't feel so bad about setting her behind up after all.

"I can't catch no bus, girl. They're waiting by the bus stop, so if I try to catch the bus home, they'll catch me. Come on, Asia. I know you ain't gon' play me like that. Your girl needs you. I'll owe you a big favor if you come get me," I pleaded.

"Okay, I'm on the way. What mall are you at again?" she asked with a sigh, knowing darn well she didn't forget that quick what mall I'd told her I was at.

"Oakland."

"I'll be there in fifteen minutes."

I flipped down my phone, and a wave of guilt overcame me. I had just set up my best friend and her father to be robbed. But my back was against the wall, and I had no choice. Where else would we get the money? Yeah, I could have hit up all the malls in the city and then flipped the merchandise for half the ticket price, but imagine how long that would have taken me. Too long. Anyway, Asia and her pops were rich, and the little money we were going to take wouldn't hurt them.

Or would it?

Minutes later, we saw Asia step out of the house and jump into her car. We watched as she pulled off and rolled off the block.

Mike pulled into their driveway and hopped out of his car. I slowly got out and looked around to make sure no one was watching. The coast was clear, so I followed Mike, who was on the porch, picking the lock. He had two paper clips stuck in the door, and he fiddled around with the locks.

I knew personally that Asia always forgot to set their house security alarm, so I wasn't really worried about that. Of course, with our luck so far, the one time she'd remember would be now.

"Hurry up," I said anxiously as I frequently glanced around.

I heard the sound of the lock clicking. I saw Mike step into the house, and I followed close behind.

I was relieved when no alarm went off. So far so good.

"Hurry up! Show me where the cash is at," Mike instructed as he scanned the spacious home.

I rushed into the living room and located the painting. I went straight to it and yelled, "It's in here."

Mike rushed over and grabbed the painting down. He pulled the lever that opened the safe, and what we got was a big surprise. The safe was empty. Not a single bill.

"Where's the cash?" he turned and asked me as if I knew. He probably realized that I was just as surprised as he was to find the safe empty once he saw how my jaw was hanging open in disbelief. Mike just shook his head as he dropped to his knees in total shock.

I put both of my hands on my head and began to pace the living room floor. Asia's father must have taken the money to the bank already. I should have known that this plan was too good to be true when the alarm didn't go off. It would have been too much like right for the money to have actually been there.

"She said that he turned in the—" Before I could even finish, I heard the sound of the door opening.

Mike and I both jumped. I dove behind the couch, and Mike froze in fear. It was Asia's father coming in.

"Hey, Asia! I'm home early," he said as he was locking the door back. At first he didn't notice Mike standing in the middle of the living room. He was too busy taking off his coat.

I didn't know what to do. When Asia's father turned around and saw Mike standing there with his safe open, he instantly reacted. He picked up the iron rod that was sitting by the living room door and got in a defensive stance.

Mike and Mr. Smith locked eyes, and they both stood there, neither of them knowing what to do next. The tension was so thick in the room, you could cut it with a knife.

I held my position behind the couch, peeking around it to watch everything unfold.

Mr. Smith looked at his open safe and then back at Mike, and he became infuriated.

"Get out of my house before I call the cops!" he yelled as he charged at Mike with the rod in hand.

Mike was just standing there like a deer in headlights. I wanted to yell out to him, "Run, fool!" but then Mr. Smith would have spotted me. Even if he hadn't spotted me, he would have recognized my voice, so I had to force myself to keep quiet as I watched Mr. Smith raise the rod at Mike.

Mr. Smith struck Mike on his head with the rod, and Mike fell to the ground. He then jumped on top of Mike and began to strike him repeatedly. That's when I saw Mike reach into his waist and pull out the shiny gun. My heart got caught in my throat. I watched fearfully as Mr. Smith continued to wildly swing the rod at Mike, not even noticing the weapon Mike now held in his hand.

Before I could say anything, I heard a big boom.

The sound echoed through the big house. I saw Mr. Smith grab his chest and gasp. I screamed as I saw Mr. Smith fall over and become motionless. Mike dropped the gun from his shaking hand, his face displaying total fear.

I ran over to Mr. Smith, but it looked like I was too late. He wasn't moving or groaning or anything.

I broke down and cried loudly. That's when panic took over. Without even thinking, I used my jacket to wipe off all the things we had touched.

I looked over at Mike. He was in shock. He hadn't moved an inch since the gun went off. He was staring at Mr. Smith's body. The look in his eyes was one that I had never seen before. He didn't even blink.

After I finished wiping the place down, I yelled, "Mike, snap out of it! Get up so we can leave!"

That boy did not budge. Not until I grabbed him and helped him up did he come to his senses.

We rushed out, both of us scared to death. A plan that was supposed to be something so simple and innocent turned out to be something much worse.

Chapter 11

Mike

My mind was telling my body to go, but it didn't move an inch. My ears were still ringing from the sound of the gun blast.

As I looked at Mr. Smith's body on the floor, I felt a pain in my heart that I had never experienced before. I could not take my eyes off of him. That's when I felt Latina helping me up off the floor. We had to get out of there quick because I had just killed a man.

The first thought that ran through my mind was of my little brothers and sister. The thought of me going to jail emerged, and the reality of what I had just done set in.

"Come on, boy!" Latina yelled as we rushed out of the house and then to my car.

Latina jumped in the driver's side, while I rode

shotgun. She knew that I was in no condition to drive. I was devastated. As weird as it might sound, I felt like I was a victim too.

I never meant to kill anybody. When Mr. Smith was on top of me, I just acted without even thinking.

The scene kept replaying over and over in my mind, and my hands couldn't stop shaking as Latina sped out of the driveway and off the street in a hurry.

Chapter 12
Twitch

That day must have been my lucky day. Almost twenty-nine thousand dollars was right in front of my eyes. I had not seen so much dough in my thirty-nine years on this earth.

Oh yeah, I forgot to introduce myself. I'm Twitch. Well, my real name is Daymond Phelps. People call me Twitch because of my jumping eye. I couldn't stop my eye from twitching if someone paid me. Ever since I developed my bad heroin addiction, I got the twitch. But enough about me. Let's get back to the money.

I was doing some drugs with my buddy Ray, and he was telling me how he had just come up on some cash. Of course, I expressed my disbelief, and that's when he led me into his bedroom, walked over to his closet, and pulled out this duffle bag. He unzipped it, and I watched as he began to thumb through the cash, bragging the whole time.

He eventually zipped up the bag and went over to this grungy chair in his room. You know how the man of the house always has a favorite chair that he comes home to sit in after a long, hard day's work? Well, this was Ray's get-high chair. Don't get me wrong, Ray and any other crackhead could get high anywhere. But there's always that favorite spot that just makes the high seem that much better.

Ray pulled out his syringe and prepared to do the drugs. I was so busy staring at the duffle bag full of money that I didn't notice when he went into convulsions. He had been doing drugs all morning, and I believe he was overdosing.

I quickly stood and began calling his name.

"Ray! Ray! Come on, man. Snap out of it" I said as I shook him.

I saw foam coming out of his mouth, and his eyes were rolling in the back of his head. I panicked and began to pace the room.

At first I was going to go call the ambulance, but I looked over at the bag of money, and greed came into play. My eyes went from my dying friend to the bag full of money, back and forth, before I finally walked over to the bag, unzipped it, and ran my hands through all of that cash myself. Right then and there, I knew what time it was. Ray was a dead man.

I know it was wrong of me to just let my friend die, but I couldn't stop thinking about the bag full of money. How I saw it, there wasn't anything I could do for Ray at that point anyway. It's not like the 9-1-1 operators provided the type of service that guests on the concierge floor of a hotel get. They didn't rush to our aid. By the time the ambulance arrived, Ray probably would have been dead.

And even if he was still alive, why prolong it by saving him, only to have him turn around and OD some other time? I had seen so many addicts overdose that I knew this was coming anyway. At least this was the excuse I used to make me feel less bad about what I was doing.

So, I did what any true crackhead would do. I took the money and ran like hell. I never had that much money in my life.

After I went to the dope house and did my thing, I headed straight to the mall. I was going to get real clean, like I used to get in the '70s. You know, like Superfly! That would show all the people on the block who had laughed at me over the years who was boss.

I went to my mother's house and stashed the money in her basement, where I had been living the past few months after a stint of homelessness. I took out a couple stacks of hundred-dollar bills and stuck them into my pocket for later because I knew, once my high went down, I would want some more dope.

I took a look in my mirror and patted my fro. I loved the new clothes I had on, but the get-up wasn't fully completed yet. So, I went to the mall and dropped three grand on a long mink coat and some lime green gators. I finally felt alive again. Twitch was back! I was about to go on the block and show off my new threads.

I was on the block telling everyone how I had just struck it big. I told everyone I hit the lottery, so they wouldn't know how I really got the money. I felt like a movie star. All of the crackhead honey dips were all over me, asking for money. I flipped through the stack of money, showing off all the hundred-dollars bills I had, and that's when it happened. A young kid grabbed me up so quick and put a gun to my head. It all happened so fast that I never saw it coming.

"Ah, brutha! What's yo' problem?" I asked as I looked in this young'un's eyes. I saw he wasn't playing and I was just hoping that he didn't pull that trigger.

The honey dips around me begin to scatter and scream when they realized the boy was holding the gun.

I just shook my head and asked myself, *Twitch, what have you gotten yourself into now?*

Chapter 13

Latina

Mike and I rode in silence around town. The vision of Mr. Smith's body kept popping up in my head. I knew Mike was thinking about the same thing. It was written all over his face.

As we rode down Woodward, we saw a crowd of people standing on the corner. They were all surrounding a man wearing a long mink coat and a pimp hat. He looked so crazy, because it was almost eighty degrees outside, and there he was with a big fur coat on. He looked like a pimp straight out of the '70s. I looked down at his shoes, anticipating two goldfish swimming around in the heels.

I saw Mike stare the man down, and then he immediately sat up in his chair.

"You see that?" Mike asked as we passed the man.

"What? That fake pimp?"

"No, that crackhead with a thousand-dollar pimp coat on. Pull over!" he said, his eyes on the man.

I pulled over to the curb, and Mike jumped out. I parked then got out and followed Mike over to the crowd.

As I got closer, I realized that the toothless man was talking about how much money he had just come up on.

Mike swiftly approached him, grabbed him by the collar, and put the gun to his neck. When the crowd of addicts saw Mike put the gun to the man, they all scattered, screaming. They did not want any part of what was about to go down. And, in all honesty, neither did I, but it was too late. I was in too deep. Way too far from the shore to swim back now.

I didn't know what Mike was thinking. Honestly, I thought he was going crazy. For the second time that day, I had seen him pull out his gun and aim it at another man. "No, Mike. Not again," I said under my breath." We were in enough trouble. One dead body on our hands was bad enough.

"Ah, brutha! What's your problem? Why you running up on me like this?" the man said as Mike pushed him up against the brick wall.

"Where did you get the money from?" Mike pressed the gun to the crackhead's neck, slightly digging into his skin.

"What money, man?" the crackhead asked, both of his hands up in the air.

Mike reached into the man's pocket and pulled out a wad of cash, mainly all hundreds.

"Where did you get this money?" Mike asked again, but this time he yelled it right in the man's ear.

"I hit the lotto!" The crackhead smiled, showing off his gums.

"Stop lying! You took it from Ray!" Mike screamed.

"Look, man, I didn't kill Ray. He was already dead when I got there. He overdosed on that stuff, man. I swear, man. Please don't kill me, man" The crackhead's entire attitude changed from that of the pimp to the ho who had just cheated her pimp out of her earnings.

"The money is at my house, man, I swear!" the crackhead continued. Afraid for his life, he spilled all the beans about what really happened.

I took a deep breath. A sense of relief came over me when he announced where the money was. But then I remembered what had just happened to Mr. Smith, and knew we had a bigger problem.

Chapter 14
Twitch

Icouldn't believe I was turning all that money over to that young boy. He made me get in the car with him and a girl while he held a gun to my head and she drove. I heard her call him by the name Mike. I don't know if that was his real name or play name. Either way it went, Mike wasn't playing! He told me to take him to the money, or he would shoot me in my leg. I had been shot before, and let me tell you . . . bullets burn!

I should have known Ray was up to no good when it came to all that money. He had probably stolen it from the young boy in the first place. It was known in the neighborhood that Ray was a professional thief. Shoot, he would steal the drawers off your behind if you weren't cautious.

I directed the young couple to my mother's house, and Mike kept the gun on me at all times. When we pulled up to the house, I noticed that nobody was home. I guess Mama had stepped out to play her lottery or something.

Mike had told his little girlfriend to wait in the car while I led him up to the house and walked through the back door. I could feel the steel barrel pressed against my back.

"Ah, brutha, you don't have to be pointing that gun on me, man. I'm too old to be trying something funny. The money is right down here in the basement," I said, hoping Mike would lighten up.

"Shut up, old man. Just take me to the money, so I can get out of here. If you give me the money, no one will get hurt." Mike gave me a stiff nudge in my back.

I led him down the stairs. I saw that my bag, the duffle bag in which Ray had kept the money, was in the middle of the couch. I could have sworn on everything that I had stuffed it under the couch. As I got closer to the bag, I could tell that someone had been in it. It was unzipped, and I was certain that I had at least zipped it back up.

"Looks like someone got in the stash," I said as I rushed over to the bag and looked in it. Most of the money was there. Only a few hundreds were peeled off. I could tell, because one of the rubber bands was popped.

I saw a note that read:

Twitch,
   I don't know what you dun got yourself into, but I borrowed five hundred dollars from this money. You owe me rent for the 20 years I've let you run in and out of my basement, so I feel I deserve it. I'm about to hit the casino!
Mama

"Ah, brutha! Don't kill me, but my mama took five hundred out of the stash. But the rest is all here," I said, scared to death. "I mean, besides what I spent on these nice-looking threads." I popped my collar, but a brutha was still scared. I just couldn't let 'im see me sweat, which was hard in this hot coat.

"How much is there?" Mike sighed, almost as if he had been expecting the worst.

I began to subtract what I had spent from the original amount. "Well, I copped some dope this morning, bought this fly coat that I'm wearing, along with my gators. That was about thirty-five hundred altogether. I found about twenty-nine thousand in the bag, so that leaves just a little over twenty-five thousand."

I saw the disappointment in the boy's eyes as he raised the gun and pointed it at me. I knew I was about to die.

Chapter 15

Latina

I waited in the car anxiously for Mike to return from the house with the money. I was sweating bullets, and the only thing I could think of was Asia's father dead back at her house on the living room floor. This had to be the worst day of my life.

I nervously tapped the steering wheel and kept my eyes on the door, expecting Mike to run out any second. As I waited, the last twenty-four hours replayed in my mind.

I should never have gone on that roof to meet Mike. If I had stayed with my girls that night, none of this would have happened. And through all of what had gone on, we still didn't have the money to give to the robbers. Those dudes seemed like they didn't play, and I was scared for my life.

I looked down at the clock and noticed that three minutes had passed. I began to worry about what was going on inside. Did the guy walk Mike into a trap? Did he really have the money? Those questions and many more went through my mind as I impatiently waited.

I felt my phone on my hip vibrate and looked at my caller ID. It was Asia calling. My mind began to race, and I felt my heart beat speed up. I didn't know if I should answer it or send her to voicemail.

The ringing finally stopped at the same time I saw Mike coming out of the house with the bag. I felt relieved when I saw him with the money. I looked at my phone again and saw that Asia had left me a voice message, but I was afraid to listen to it.

Chapter 16

Mike

I rushed out of the house with the twenty-five thousand dollars. I knew I was five G's short, but at least I got most of the money back.

When I jumped in the car, I noticed the worried look in Latina's eyes. I had put her in a terrible situation with the shooting, and I felt so bad for it. She looked like she felt better, though, when I showed her the bag full of money.

"I got it!" I said as I put the money in the backseat. The only thing I had to do now was get it to the two robbers. They had threatened my family, and I could not risk their lives for any amount of money.

In one day, I had committed a murder, held someone at gunpoint, and broken into someone's house.

Although I was still a minor, the crimes I'd committed that day alone would land me a lifetime in jail.

"I can't wait until this nightmare is finally over," I said as I leaned back in my seat and we pulled off.

"I can't wait either. I wish this day had never happened," Latina said as she drove.

For the first time, I noticed how beautiful Latina really was. I mean, I always thought she was attractive, but now that I really got to know her, she was more than just attractive.

And, on top of that, she didn't bail out on me. Even after I shot her friend's father, she didn't leave me out to dry alone. She was a down chick. She could have been done left me alone to handle the situation by myself, but she stuck by me. That alone was a beautiful thing.

"You know, you're not so bad, Latina. I hate that it took these bad circumstances for us to spend some time with each other."

"Yeah. What a first date, huh?" she said as she put on a forced smile.

I could tell that Latina was rattled, and I couldn't blame her.

I told her to take me home so I could check on my family. I remained quiet the whole ride home, and Latina didn't say a word either. I saw the tears in her eyes and knew that she felt the same way I did—horrible.

* * *

When we pulled up to my house, I noticed a car parked in my driveway that I had never seen before. "I'll be right back," I said as I got out of the car and headed into the house with the duffle bag in hand.

I heard my little brothers and sister laughing. I walked in and saw the two men that had approached me earlier playing with them. My heart dropped at the sight of them around my family. They were laughing and playing UNO.

My grandmother sat at the table with a big smile on her face. She was the first to speak.

"Oh, there you are, baby," Big Mama greeted me. "These nice men are here from your high school and said that you were picked for a summer program. They have been waiting to talk to you," she said excitedly.

My grandmother seemed so happy to tell me the news. Little did she know, they were two bank robbers who had threatened our lives.

I immediately put on a fake smile and told my little brothers and sister to go upstairs and play.

"But I want to play with them. They are so fun!" one of my little brothers said as he jumped around wildly.

"No! Go upstairs!" I grabbed his hand and pulled him away from the man.

My grandmother stood up and gathered the kids. "Let's leave Mike-Mike alone to talk to these nice men, okay?" Big Mama tugged my brother and sister away. "It was nice meeting you two gentlemen." She shook their hands.

"It was nice meeting you too. We'll take good care of your grandson. He is such a nice young boy," the taller and skinnier of the two men said as he shot me a fake smile.

My grandma turned to me and gave me a big hug. "I'm so proud of you, Mike-Mike. I'll let you talk to them. We'll be upstairs," she said just before she, along with the kids, left the room.

As soon as my grandmother was out of sight, I pulled out my gun, but not soon enough. One of the men grabbed it out of my hand and punched me dead in the face. I stumbled to the ground, and they both began to laugh.

"What do you think you doing, li'l punk? Do you think you're dealing with rookies or something?" the tall, skinny man said. "Where's our money?" He put my gun in his waistband.

"It's in the bag," I mumbled as I got up and wiped the blood dripping from my lip. "There's only twenty-five grand in the bag, but that's all I have. You don't know the trouble I had to go through to get that money back," I said as I watched the skinny man walk over to the bag and look in it. "Now get out my house. You have your money!"

"Where's the other five grand?" the skinny man said as he sifted through the bag.

"A crackhead spent it, man. You lucky I was able to even get that back. Just take your money and leave," I said as I pointed at the door.

The two men came walking toward me. The fat man grabbed me by my collar and said, "Where's the rest of the money, punk? You must want me to take a visit up those stairs to your sweet little grandmother, huh?"

"No. I don't have the money. Please don't hurt my family. They have nothing to do with this," I pleaded.

"If we don't have the rest of our money by midnight, we're coming back here, and it won't be to play UNO," the skinny man said before he and his partner headed out with the bag and slammed the door.

I fell to my knees. My whole world was crumbling down. How was I going to get another five thousand dollars?

Chapter 17
Latina

I watched as the two men who had approached us earlier came out of Mike's place and got in a car that was parked in the driveway. I got worried, not knowing what they might have possibly done to Mike and his family while they were in there. I saw them with the duffle bag, so hopefully, the nightmare was over.

I watched as they pulled off. Then I heard my phone ring again. I looked down at the caller ID, and once again, it was Asia. I didn't have the courage to pick up, so I sent her to voice mail.

I saw Mike coming out of the house with a bloody lip. I knew something had gone wrong. I got out of the car and ran to him.

"Are you okay? What did they do to you?" I asked as I put my hands on his cheeks.

"I'm cool, but I have some bad news. They're still not letting up. They said I have to come up with the other five grand by the end of the night," Mike explained as he brushed past me and got into the driver's seat of the car. "They threatened my family, and I can't let that happen. I have to do what I have to do. You can dip on me now if you want, but with or without you, I gotta make a move." Mike stared at me momentarily, as if waiting on a response. "So, what's it going to be?"

Without even hesitating, I replied, "Let's do this then."

The sun had gone down, and Mike and I only had a couple of hours to get the rest of the money. Mike was desperate, and I could see it in his eyes.

I couldn't believe we were breaking into another place. This time it was Mr. Johnson's gym. Mike knew that Mr. Johnson had a habit of not locking the back door, and as luck would have it, it was unlocked.

We crept in. The place was in complete darkness. Mike told me earlier that Mr. Johnson frequently kept money in his office, and we were just going to borrow it. I had a bad feeling about it, but we had no choice.

We crept to the back of the building to Mr. Johnson's office, and I followed Mike in. Mike headed straight for the desk and pulled open the drawer. He reached in and pulled out a small metal box.

"This is where he keeps the cash," Mike whispered.

He opened the box and began to search through it. Seconds later, he pulled out a wad of cash. "Bingo!" he said.

All of a sudden, the lights came on, and we saw Mr. Johnson standing in the doorway. We both froze in fear. Mr. Johnson had a bat in his hands.

"What are you doing, Mike?" he asked in a disappointed tone.

Mike dropped the money and stood there speechless. "Mr. Johnson, I just was going to borrow it," he said. "I was going to pay you back, work it off or something."

Mr. Johnson looked heartbroken. It was an awkward silence as we all stood there. At this point, I knew we were going to jail.

At least the nightmare would be over.

Chapter 18
Luke and Goon

Luke and Goon drove away from Mike's house with most of the money in the duffle bag.

"Luke, let's just hit another bank to get the rest of the money for Li'l Luke," Goon suggested, trying to ease his brother's dilemma.

"No, Goon. I told you that I wasn't doing any more robbing after that bank job. I just want the rest of the money for Li'l Luke's surgery," Luke said.

Luke pulled out the gun he got from Mike and looked at it. He didn't want the lifestyle that he had, but he knew it was his only way. He had spent five years of his life in jail, and didn't want to go back. He knew by robbing and stealing, he would make his way back there before long.

Luke gave Mike until midnight to have his money,

or he would have to do what he had to do. He didn't want to hurt Mike, but he knew he had to provide for his son.

"Let's celebrate!" Goon said as he stared at the bag full of money.

"There's nothing to celebrate about, bro. This money is stolen, and the only reason I'm keeping it is for my son," Luke said as his conscience began to come into play. He felt bad about all he did to get the money.

Since his last stint in jail, he had promised his old lady that he'd keep his nose clean, that he'd never do anything else that would jeopardize him being with his family. And even though he felt justified in his last criminal activity, he knew from that point on he had to keep his promise.

"Well, at least let me have a little fun. Drop me off at the bar around the corner from your house," Goon said. He was a heavy drinker and loved to get drunk.

"Okay, but don't get too wasted up there, bro. We still have business to handle tonight. I think I'm about to go home and rest until eleven thirty. I'll pick you up when I go to meet the boy to get the rest of the money."

After Luke instructed his brother to pinch a couple hundred dollars from the bag, he dropped off his brother at the bar and pulled away.

Unfortunately, he didn't see the oncoming truck as he merged into traffic. At sixty miles per hour, the truck crashed into his car and spun him out of control. His car totaled, Luke lay unconscious on his steering wheel.

Chapter 19

Mike

I sat across from Mr. Johnson and finished explaining to him all that happened that day and the previous night on the rooftop of his gym. I told him the whole story about the money and me shooting Asia's father. Mr. Johnson was very disappointed in me and told me that I never had to steal from him. He said all I had to do was ask him. I felt so low at that point, but I hadn't seen any other way to get the money. My family's wellbeing was on the line.

I listened as Mr. Johnson tried to help me with our situation.

"Mike, you shot a man and left him there to die," he started. "You have to turn yourself in. I have a friend that's a detective for the police department. I'm going to give him a call, so he can help you out.

And you don't have to worry about getting any money to those bad guys. He'll know what to do." Mr. Johnson put his hand on my shoulder.

Latina was sitting right next to me, and I heard her phone ring.

"It's Asia," she said just before she took a deep breath and answered her phone.

I waited patiently for her to get off the phone. I knew Asia was probably calling to tell her that someone had killed her father.

While Latina was listening to Asia on the phone, she was quiet. Asia told her something that made her face go pale. It looked like Latina had seen a ghost or something.

Latina closed the phone with a look of disbelief on her face before saying, "Mr. Smith is still alive. He's at the hospital in stable condition. He survived the shooting."

Chapter 20

Luke

Luke sat in the hospital bed with bandages over his head. He was grateful that he had only sustained what he considered minor injuries in the car crash. He was non-responsive when the ambulance first arrived on the scene, but then he quickly came to. He was taken to the hospital and given X-rays, just as a precaution. The treating doctor found that he had a concussion, and therefore wanted to keep him in the hospital a couple days for observation. Luke didn't want to be sitting up in the hospital, especially since he had unfinished business to take care of, but the doctor insisted.

Even when Luke told the doctor he didn't have insurance to cover the bill, the doctor smiled and told him, "Trust me, most of the people who I treat in the

ER don't have insurance, but that doesn't mean they don't deserve to be made well."

Luke couldn't believe the compassion this stranger was showing him. If only all those people he had done job interviews for had showed that kind of compassion, maybe he wouldn't be in this predicament in the first place.

Although Luke knew he had to get the rest of his cash from Mike, the only thing he could think about now was how close he had come to death. He would have left his wife and son alone if he had been killed. He began to rethink his life of crime and his destructive lifestyle.

"Ugh!" Luke heard someone say.

He looked over at the man in the hospital bed next to him. The man didn't look so good. He had a bandage around his chest, but he was awake, moaning and groaning.

"What are you in for?" Luke asked the man, trying to make small talk.

"I walked in on an intruder breaking into my house. He shot me in the shoulder when I caught him. The doctor said the bullet went in and out. He says I'm lucky to be alive." The man looked down at his wound. "Tell my shoulder that, though. It hurts like heck."

"Seems like we're both having bad days, huh?" Luke said, in an attempt to ease up the mood.

"I suppose. Then again, I hate to admit it, but finally finding some time to rest instead of always being on my feet running around, making sure my restaurants are running okay just might do me some good." The man let out a chuckle. "Guess this is the man upstairs way of setting my tail down."

Luke looked upward, wondering if maybe God was trying to tell him something too.

"So, what brought you here?" the man asked Luke.

Luke told his roommate about the accident and his injuries.

The two men ended up talking for hours and found out that they had a lot in common—but they had no idea how closely they were connected. The man who sat next to Luke was Asia's father. Luke had no idea that, in a way, he was responsible for Mr. Smith getting shot. Had Luke not threatened Mike to come up with the missing portion of the robbery money, Mike and Latina never would have been in Mr. Smith's house committing the crime that resulted in Mr. Smith's injury.

By the time Luke was released from the hospital, which was a couple of days before Mr. Smith's release, he had a guaranteed position waiting for him at one of Mr. Smith's pizza parlors. Mr. Smith had even promised to give him an advance on his pay to help toward Li'l Luke's surgery.

Once again, someone had shown Luke compassion. Luke felt like the happiest man in the world. He didn't even think about going after Mike for the money anymore. He finally had a chance to make the money the right way.

Chapter 21

Latina

A few days after Mr. Smith was shot and hospitalized, Mike and I found ourselves sitting down at the police station with Mr. Johnson. As promised, he had put in a call to his detective friend. After giving his friend all the details of what Mike had shared with him (without giving him Mike's or my name), his friend promised he'd put in a word so that the judge would go easy on us if we turned ourselves in.

Mike was hesitant at first, as the detective couldn't make any engraved-in-stone promises regarding jail time. Mike feared leaving his family to have to fend for themselves, so he wanted to weigh his options. Was it worth it to turn himself in, or better not to, and then run the risk of being caught? If we were caught, a judge might slap us with heavy time behind bars. Maybe turning ourselves in would make the judge more lenient, and we could get little to no jail time. While Mike took a day to sleep on it, I came up with an idea that I thought might even help us out more.

"Mr. Smith," I said as I stood at the side of his hospital bed.

When I'd first entered the room, I almost punked out. I stood outside of the partly opened curtain, trying to maintain the courage that had brought me down to the hospital in the first place.

"Latina? Is that you?" he said. "I thought I heard someone. My roommate left a few days ago, so I wasn't sure if I was hearing things."

"No, you're not hearing things, Mr. Smith," I told him. "Can I come in?"

"Sure, sweetie." He looked over my shoulder. "Where's Asia? Is she parking the car or something?"

Mr. Smith had assumed I was up there with Asia, but I wasn't. Still, I wasn't alone.

"Uh, I'm not here with Asia, Mr. Smith. But I did bring someone along with me."

Upon hearing his cue, Mike entered the room. He'd been standing outside of the door.

"Uh, Mr. Smith, this is Mike," I introduced. "Mike, this is Mr. Smith, Asia's father."

Mike couldn't even look the man in the eyes as he shook Mr. Smith's hand.

Noticing Mike's demeanor, Mr. Smith asked, "Latina, what's this all about?"

I proceeded to tell Mr. Smith the exact same story Mike had told Mr. Johnson. At the time, I didn't know how much good it was going to do. I didn't know if he was going to holler out to the nurses to call the police and have us arrested right there on the spot. But, lo and behold, Mr. Smith was more understanding than I think I would have been.

Mike was glad that he'd taken my advice for us to go to Mr. Smith and explain to him what happened before going to the police. In doing so, Mr. Smith decided not to press charges against us, thank God, but he told us we had to admit to breaking and entering. Better that than attempted murder.

In addition to that, Mr. Smith said he expected us to pay restitution, off the record, by putting in work at his parlors. Mike and I gladly agreed.

So now, here we sat at the police station, retelling our story to Mr. Johnson's detective friend face to face.

After we finished, the detective left the room and then returned about twenty minutes later. The news was not so good, but it was better than it could have been. According to the detective, it would be a while before Mike and I could begin keeping our promise to Mr. Smith because, even though he decided he wouldn't press charges against us, the state had no choice but to pick up the charges.

Mike and I were arrested on the spot, but since we were both juveniles with clean records, we were let out on our own recognizance.

Mr. Johnson got in touch with my mother and Mike's grandmother, filling them in on all of the details while they waited down at the station to sign us out. Whether or not my mom was high before she got there was beyond me, but my being brought out in handcuffs and released right before her eyes sobered her up real quick.

My heart raced a mile a minute when my mom came charging toward me. I thought she was going to knock my block off, but instead, she simply embraced me and said, "I'm so sorry, Tina. This is all my fault. I should have been there for you. I should have been a better mother. I promise you, from this day forward, I'm gonna do better. I see where you're heading, and it ain't a good place. But like Mr. Johnson here said"—My mother turned to Mr. Johnson, who was sitting and waiting with Mike's grandmother for him to come out. "It's never too late. You still got a chance to do better than me. And I'm going to see to it that you do."

It took everything in me not to break down right then and there in that police station. I just might have if, seconds later, Mike hadn't come around the corner. I'd been a ride-or-die chick up to this point, so I wasn't about to let him see me looking soft. But the way Mike broke down with his grandmother as they embraced, it was obvious that he couldn't care less what he looked like in front of me. That's when, for the first time, I truly understood why he'd made all the choices he'd made over the last few days. And if I was seeing things right, he'd do it all again. And I can't lie. If it meant giving my mother a long-needed wake-up call, then the same would go for me.

Needless to say, those dudes who had robbed the bank didn't even show back up to try to get at Mike and me. I guess their conscience took over and they decided not to come after us for the rest of the money. Or maybe they were dead or something; got shot trying to rob another bank. Who knows? All I know is, they weren't our problem anymore.

I learned more life lessons in that little bit of time than I had learned in my entire lifetime. And if I didn't learn anything else, I learned that karma is real, and what goes around comes around.

Mike and I should have never taken that money, because it was not ours. Because of it, people overdosed, got shot, and we had to lie and steal.

Asia's father had a good heart to forgive us, but as I walked out of that police station, I thought about how I could have prevented all the bad things from happening in the first place.

The detective later told me that the money stolen from the bank was mysteriously returned by an unnamed person, and enclosed was a note saying that he was sorry. I knew who the letter was from, and I guessed that those two robbers must have had a change of heart about a lot of things.

Despite my mother's plea in the police station, she still uses drugs, and I don't know how I can help her. I've come to the conclusion, though, that she really has to want to help herself. It's not something she can do for me. She has to want to do it for her. But she's still my moms, and I still love her to death. I just hope that someday, if I ever have a daughter, I can be a better example in her life. So, in order to do that, I know there are some things I have to change. Starting now . . . or even tomorrow because, like Mr. Johnson said, it's never too late.

Note from the Author

Latina was sentenced to three years in Detroit's Detention Home for Girls. She is currently 19 and attends a major university in Michigan. Mike also received three years, and after his release, he turned his life around. He is now the legal guardian for his younger brothers and sister, due to the passing of Big Mama.

Luke finally got his life on track and is a district manager at a major pizza chain in Detroit. He was able to pay for Li'l Luke's surgery, and is living a happy life with his family.

Asia, well, you can read about her in another Babygirl Drama. Her story is going to blow you away.

Remember, life is what you make it. It's all about choices. At some point in your life, you will approach a fork in the road, and it's your decision to choose the right or wrong path.

Babygirl Daniels

Sneak Peek of Volume 3: Sister Sister

Chapter One

My name is Tara Evans, and if someone were to examine my life, they would think that I had it good. I live in Southfield, Michigan, a nice suburban area right outside of Detroit. My family is what some might consider paid. Both my mother and father work for General Motors, and in Michigan, that equals affluence and success.

Out of all my friends, I'm the only one who has two parents living under the same roof, so I guess some could consider me fortunate, but I don't quite see it that way. See, I have to share my parents because I'm not an only child. I'm a twin, and although everybody thinks it is so cool to have one, let me be the first to tell you, it's not.

Physically, my sister Mya and I are identical in

every way. We have the same chestnut-colored skin, the same hair length and texture, and the same honey-brown eyes. You'd think that since we were so much alike, everyone would treat us the same, but I noticed a difference even from my own parents when I was only five.

Mya had always been the popular twin. She was the one that people gravitated to. People liked her and wanted to be around her. They didn't necessarily exclude me, but they only included me because of Mya. Invitations to birthday parties and other social events always had Mya's name on it first. I almost felt like people said, "You might as well invite her sister too."

Even my parents put her first. They catered to her as if she were their little china doll, giving her any and everything she asked for. Even something so small as Mya sitting in the front seat while I was stuck in the back bothered me. I don't think that my parents even realized that they did this, but it didn't stop it from hurting all the same.

They were harder on me than they were on her. If I brought home a bad grade from school, then they were down my throat, telling me that I could do better, but if Mya happened to slip up once or twice, they were very understanding.

It may sound like I'm whining, but I'm not. It was

unfair that I had to live in my sister's shadow. I had wanted to be my own person for so long that sometimes I just wanted to scream, "What about me?"

I felt neglected by my parents, invisible to my friends, and unimportant in general. Mya's life was so great that I couldn't help but feel jealous. Please don't get me wrong. I loved my sister. I could see why everyone worshiped the ground she walked on. She was amazing. Besides being gorgeous, she was confident. She had a diva complex that fit her perfectly, and she dressed as if she had stepped off the front cover of a magazine.

I admired her and wished that we could switch personalities. I wanted what she had. I wanted people to see me and think of me as the "it girl."

Mya was known all the way from Southfield to Inkster. Everyone in and out of Detroit knew her. Even kids from other schools knew who she was. Her reputation preceded her, and I wished that I knew what it felt like to be in her shoes.

Summer vacation was winding down, and everybody was excited about going back to school. Mya and I had one last thing on the agenda before we could focus on returning to tests and study groups: We had to plan our seventeenth birthday party. Well, Mya did most of the planning because she basically had the entire shindig mapped out in her head before we even sat down with our parents. My mom and dad didn't even notice that Mya was making all the decisions, until the entire thing was already planned.

"Oh, is there something that you want to add, Tara? Everything is already done, but I'm sure we can rearrange some things if you have some ideas," my father said.

"No," Mya whined. "If anything gets added, it will take away from the party. It will be perfect, Tara, I promise." She turned to me and put her arms around my neck as she kissed my cheek repeatedly. "Please, please, just let me plan our party this year. Next year you can do the entire thing. I pinky swear."

It was a pinky swear that she had broken since we were ten years old. Like I said before, she always got her way, and I was always left with no opinion or voice of my own.

"It's fine, Daddy," I replied quietly, a disappointed look on my face. "May I be excused?" I asked as I stood.

My mother looked toward my father and then at Mya before responding, "Sure, sweetheart. You're excused. Are you sure you don't have any ideas? I'm sure Mya won't mind if you add just a couple."

Add a couple? I thought angrily. *You didn't give Mya a limit to the amount of things she could add.* "No, it's her party. She can plan it."

As I walked away toward my room, I had to brush a tear from my cheek.

I don't think Mya tried to be selfish. I blamed my parents. They had created such a drastic difference between the two of us for so long that everybody assumed that Mya was the better twin. They had placed her on a pedestal, and no matter what I did, I couldn't compete. That was not how a sisterhood was supposed to be. I knew that I shouldn't feel like I had to compete for attention and love with my own sister, but I did.

Mya came bouncing into the room. She sat down on my bed and handed me a long list of names.

"What is this?" I asked dryly.

"The guest list. Daddy said that I had to run it by you," she replied.

I looked over the list. All one hundred names were people that I knew, but most of them were Mya's fans. One name in particular caused a smile to cross my face.

"What are you smiling at?" Mya asked as a wicked smile crossed her own face. "You must be looking at Maurice's name," she teased. "I know you like him."

"I don't like him. I don't even really know him, Mya. I've only seen him around," I insisted. I didn't want her to know I had a schoolgirl's crush on Maurice.

He was a young thug around our neighborhood. He was our age, but he rarely went to school. The only time I saw him was when he was trying to show off something new—shoes, jewelry, or even a car that he had. I knew he was bad news.

Although my sister and I had permission to date, my parents would never allow me to leave the house with him in a million years. As soon as he pulled up in his old-school Monte Carlo with the speakers knocking, my daddy would have chased him away without hesitation.

"Yeah, okay, Tara. You ain't fooling anybody. I'll hook you up if you want me to. You know he's Asia's half brother."

"I told you I wasn't feeling him like that, My-My," I said, using the nickname I had given her as a child. "So leave it alone."

"Okay. But when one of these girls out here takes your man from right underneath your nose, don't say I didn't tell you to get on him first." She laughed as she snatched the list from my hands. "So, are you gonna add any names or what?"

"No, I think you got it covered. I'll just show up," I stated.

"It's going to be the hottest party of the year!" Mya was excited. I could tell because it was all she had talked about since the beginning of the summer. Now that the party was only a week away, she was like a kid who could not wait for Christmas to arrive.

"By the way, what are you wearing?"

"I don't know. I'm going to just wear something I already have, I guess," I replied nonchalantly. The party had become an all-about-Mya affair. I really didn't think it mattered what I wore. Everything was going to revolve around her anyway. I would be surprised if she put my name on the cake.

"No, you are not going to wear something old. This is our birthday. We have to be the best-dressed girls there. I know you want to look cute for Maurice," she sang, as if that would make me change my mind. "You should ask Daddy to buy us new outfits."

"Why me? You're the one who he can't tell no," I stated sarcastically.

"I know, but you have to warm him up. Once he tells you no, he'll think about it for a minute and feel bad. Once I go back and ask him again, he's sure to say yes. So go hurry up and ask him," she urged.

I don't think she even knew how bossy she was. It was just her personality, and I was used to it. The fact that my father could tell me no and turn around and tell her yes bothered me, but I did want a new outfit, so I went along with Mya's plan.

My parents were sitting in the dining room looking over the bill from the party planner that they had allowed Mya to hire. I sensed something was wrong, and that this was the wrong time to be asking for something, but if I went back upstairs, Mya would only usher me back down, so I got it out of the way.

"Daddy," I said, "can I have some money to buy a new outfit for the party?"

My father stood up and approached me. "Sweetheart, I wish I could. Things are kind of tight right now. My job is not as stable as it used to be, and your sister has already gone over budget with this party for the two of you. Can you just wear something out of your closet for Daddy?"

His answer would not have been so heartbreaking if I had not known that he would turn around and tell Mya yes. I wondered what was so much better about my sister that made my parents love her more, and my eyes started to tear, but I blinked them away.

"Sure, Daddy. I'll wear something in my closet. I have some cute stuff anyway," I answered.

He kissed my forehead and replied, "That's my girl. I love you, sweetheart."

"I love you too," I replied.

I went back upstairs, and as soon as I entered my room, Mya stated, "Did he say no yet, or did he hit you with the 'I'll think about it'?"

"He said no," I answered. "He always says no."

"Okay, well, let me show you how it's done, sis."

Mya got up to leave as I sat down on my bed. She didn't know how much it hurt to be the twin that no one cared about.

If she knew what it was like to be me, she wouldn't throw stuff in my face so much.

I knew that my sister was not a bad person. Selfish, yes; arrogant, yes; but I couldn't see her intentionally hurting my feelings. At least I hoped she would never do the things that she did on purpose.

I crept out of my room and stood at the top of the stairs to see what my father would tell Mya.

"Didn't your sister just ask for a new outfit?" I heard my mother say. "I know she told you what your father said."

I knew that they had to be stressed over money, because our mother didn't usually speak to Mya in such a harsh tone. She was just as bad, if not worse than Daddy, when it came to spoiling my sister.

"That's all right, Monica." My father interrupted my mother. "How much money do you need, Mya?" he asked.

What? My brain screamed in rage and jealousy. When I asked, he was broke. Now, just because it was Mya, he suddenly had money. *Favoritism* was not the word to describe how differently my father treated us.

"Three hundred," Mya replied.

She was so spoiled. She stood with one hand on her hip and the other hand stuck out, waiting for our father to place the bills inside. Mya really did act like money grew on trees, and the fact that my parents gave her no limits was a part of the problem.

I watched as my father went into his wallet and pulled out some money. He counted the bills and then handed it to Mya. "Here's four hundred," he said. "Two hundred for you and two for your sister. That's the best I can do right now, honey. I'm sorry."

I could not believe my ears. He was actually apologizing to her for not giving her the three hundred dollars she had originally asked for. How bogus was that? He had told me no without hesitating. There was no thinking about it or empty promises. It was like he did not mind disappointing me, but would do anything to please Mya. And if finances were as tight as he had told me they were, he was willing to put us in the poor house just to buy her a new blouse.

"Thank you, Daddy," Mya said and then ran up the stairs, where I stood with my arms folded. She handed two hundred dollars to me. "We're going shopping tomorrow."

"Whoopee," I replied as I rolled my eyes and twirled my finger.

"Well, if you don't want to, you can wear something old, and I'll go by myself," she shot back.

"I'm just tired, Mya, that's all. Thanks for getting the money," I said.

We went into our room and retired for the night. I couldn't believe my father. How could he love one child more than another? It was cruel to me, and the more he and my mother treated Mya like she was better than me, the more I began to believe that it had to be the truth.

Chapter Two

The next day, Mya and I picked up our friends, Summer and Asia, before we headed to the mall. We all wanted to look good at the party. It would be the biggest blowout of the year. Even better than the party this dude named Mike had thrown earlier this summer. And our clique had to be the best dressed there.

We were all really cool, but I liked Summer best. Sometimes I liked her even better than my sister.

Summer and I had met through Mya, of course, a year before, when she transferred to Cass High. At first I thought she was just like everybody else who we hung around. She and Mya became fast friends, but a big misunderstanding caused them to fall out, and they hadn't been the same since.

Ever since then, Summer and I had gotten closer. She was my best friend. In fact, I felt like she was one of my only true friends, because she liked me for me and not because of my sister.

We all headed into Somerset Mall. Why Mya drove to the most expensive mall in Michigan was beyond me. We only had $200 each to spend, and at Somerset that would not stretch very far.

"Why didn't you go to Northland Mall?" I asked Mya.

"Because I don't want to be wearing the same stuff that every other ghetto girl is going to be wearing. If we get our outfits from there, then at least five other people will have on our stuff. Can't nobody afford to shop at Somerset," Mya bragged.

"Including y'all," Asia added playfully. "Didn't you say your daddy only gave you a few hundred bucks?"

"Don't worry about me," Mya stated. "You just worry about what you're wearing, because my outfit gon' be on point. I promise you."

I smirked as I watched Summer roll her eyes toward the sky. Everybody in the car was used to Mya's arrogance. She had to be the most conceited teenage girl in the world—a young girl with a grown woman attitude. She thought she was the next Naomi Campbell, and she treated people almost as badly as the esteemed supermodel.

I couldn't understand why people loved her so much and simply put up with me. I tried to be nice and act down-to-earth. Maybe if I acted like a you-know-what, then people would like me as much as they did Mya.

We climbed out of the car. Ironically, I rode in the backseat of the car that my parents had purchased for both me and Mya. Yeah, right. She wasn't even willing to share my parents' attention, so I knew her sharing a car was out of the question.

"I think I'm going to walk around for a bit," Summer said as she headed toward the south end of the mall. "Call me on my cell if you guys need to find me."

"Wait up! I'll go with you," I called out.

I walked away with Summer, while Asia and Mya headed into the Prada store, Mya with only $200 to her name. Asia, on the other hand, might have had enough in her pocketbook to purchase something from the Prada store. Because her father owned a popular pizza chain, she pretty much kept money. She was cocky with hers, not as cocky as Mya, but still, they made the perfect pair.

"You ready for your party?" Summer asked me.

"Come on now," I said with a weak smile. "It may be my birthday, but you know that this is far from my party."

Most people loved when their birthdays rolled

around. It was the one day when they were granted a pass and everything was about them. I never knew what that felt like. Being a twin, I never had anything to myself. I always shared everything with Mya. Our birthday was never about me.

When we were younger, after my mother and father put me to bed, they would give Mya an extra gift. Every year it happened like clockwork. The first year I discovered what they were doing was when I was five. I had gotten up to use the bathroom, and I heard my mother talking to my sister in their bedroom. When I peeked through the door, I saw them handing her a gift. I was confused, because I thought that we had opened all of our birthday presents, but obviously they had saved the best gift for the best girl.

I watched my sister open up her present and pull out a gold necklace. My mother had always told me that we were too young to wear jewelry, but I guess her rules did not apply to Mya. My tiny heart was broken in pieces that night, and it was that day I concluded that my mom and dad loved Mya more.

"Hey, you should enjoy your party too," Summer said.

I think she could sense my distress. I was always so good at masking my feelings, but I had gotten so comfortable with Summer that I didn't feel the need to lie to her. "It is your birthday."

"Yeah, you're right. It just feels like everything is always about Mya. I'm used to it, though," I admitted.

Summer stopped walking and put her hands on her hips. "I've got an idea," she said excitedly.

"What?"

"Let's forget about your party," she suggested.

"What? You're crazy. Do you know how much money my daddy has put into this thing?"

"So?" she shot back. "Was any of that money for you? You said that it's always about Mya, so why even show up? Maybe if you decide to spend your birthday somewhere else, then they'll finally see that they treat you unfairly."

I thought about it for a moment. I guess it really didn't matter whether I went to the party. I could skip it this year. The entire guest list was written by Mya anyway, and I was almost positive that she had planned everything to revolve around her. The entire world revolved around her.

Why not? I deserve to do what I want and be around my real friends on my birthday. Sometimes I have to make things about me, I thought.

"What are we going to do? Everybody in Detroit will be at the party. Where are we going to go?" I asked.

"Anywhere you want to," Summer replied. "We can

go out to eat or just do something small. Whatever we do, it will be about you and only you, not your sister. I'll even bake you a cake."

"I wouldn't be wrong for skipping out on Mya?" I asked unsurely. I didn't want my sister to think that I didn't want to be around her. We had never been apart on our birthday, but the more I thought about it, the more I doubted that she would even notice.

"You would be right for doing it, T. It's about time you stopped letting Mya steal your shine, girl. Take one day for yourself. It'll be fun," Summer insisted.

I smiled. It was good to know I had one person in my life who had my back. The type of friendship I had with her was the same type that I wanted to have with Mya, but I knew that, if in seventeen years we had not developed a friendship, we probably never would.

"You would do that for me?" I asked.

"Tara, please, after everything you did for me last year when my sister died . . . I owe you. You were the only person I could count on. We're friends, and that's what friends do for each other," she said as she wrapped her arm around my shoulder. "Now, let's go find you an outfit for *your* special day."

It took me and Summer two hours to bargain shop and find something that I could afford in the expensive mall. I was grateful for the release. When we were together, I didn't feel like the unpopular twin. I just felt like a regular teenage girl.

Summer and I were getting ready to sit down for a bite to eat in the food court when my cell phone rang. I checked the caller ID.

"Here's the queen bee now," I said playfully.

"See if they're ready to meet up," Summer said.

"Hello," I answered.

"Hey, Tara," Mya greeted.

"Hey, where are you? Summer and I are almost done. Are you and Asia ready to meet up yet? Did you find something to wear?" I asked.

"Oh yeah, I found something," Mya replied distractedly.

I could hear a horn honking in the background, and I frowned. "Where are you? What's that noise? It sounds like you're outside," I stated.

"Listen, that's why I called you. I had to leave the mall. Can y'all meet me up the block?"

"What do you mean you had to leave the mall?"

Summer frowned her face and asked, "She left us here?"

I put my hand over the receiver of the cell phone and informed Summer about what was going on. "She wants us to meet her up the street." I then removed my hand from the phone.

"What's going on?" I asked Mya. "Just come back and pick us up."

Before Mya could respond, three security guards ran up on Summer and me, interrupting my call.

"You need to come with us," one of the guards stated as he grabbed my arm firmly and lifted me from my seat, causing me to drop my phone.

"What are you doing? Come with you for what?" I asked as I snatched my arm away.

Summer jumped up. "Let her go!"

I tried to struggle against the guards, but that only caused them to get rougher. They pulled out mace and sprayed my face. My eyes burned furiously, and I went blind temporarily, everything turning gray as my eyes felt like they were having a seizure.

"What did you do that for? What are you doing? She didn't do anything," I heard Summer yell.

"Summer, call my parents!" I yelled as I felt myself being dragged off.

The guards pulled me into the security office and sat me in a chair.

"Where is the merchandise that you stole?" they asked me.

"What are you talking about?" I asked. My eyes were watering profusely. I couldn't stop them. They were running like faucets. "My eyes are burning! I need to rinse them out!"

"Water makes it worse. If you tell us what you did with the clothes that you stole, we can let you go. All you have to do is return them, and no charges will be pressed," another guard explained.

"Didn't I tell you I don't know what you're talking about!" I screamed.

They opened the door, and a young white woman walked into the room. I could barely see her because my eyes were hurting so badly.

"Is this her?" the guard asked the woman.

"Yeah, that's her. I saw her with my own eyes. The camera system is out this week, so the managers have us watching the entire store closely. She stole the clothes," the woman said in a matter-of-fact tone.

It wasn't until I actually thought about it that I realized that they thought I was Mya. That had to be the only explanation, because the lady sounded positive that she was identifying the right person. She didn't know that I was a twin. It was a case of mistaken identity. That's why Mya and Asia left the mall so abruptly. She almost got caught shoplifting. Now here I was taking the fall for something I didn't do.

I knew that I could not give my sister up. I was filled with rage that Mya would even leave me at the scene of one of her crimes, but I wouldn't snitch on her. I didn't think that she meant for me to get caught instead of her, but she should have never left the mall without me. That was grimy and inconsiderate in it-self, because if the shoe was on the other foot, I would have never left her.

"You know that if you don't cooperate with us, the store will press criminal charges. This will go on your criminal record," a guard told me.

I heard them, and my heart beat faster from the intensity inside the room, but there was nothing I could do but sit there and take the heat. Mya had done me dirty, but I couldn't bring myself to return the favor. So I sat silently and waited for my parents to arrive.

I knew that they would be upset. I had never been in trouble before, so the fact that they would be getting a call like this would come as a complete surprise.

"We need to contact your parents. What is a number where we can reach them?" a guard asked me.

I kept my head down and gave him the number.

The rest of the guards left the room along with the store clerk, leaving me there with the guard who was making the call. I was more afraid of what my parents would think of me than anything else. I hated to disappoint them, even though they always disappointed me.

The guard hung up the phone, and I looked up at him.

"I didn't get an answer. Now, I'm going to give you

one more chance to tell me where you put the merchandise. If you don't, I won't have a choice but to
hand you over to the city police. We can't hold you
here," the guard stated, trying to play nice.

I remained silent. There was nothing left to say.

When the police finally arrived after the guard
kept his promise and called them, I was handcuffed
like a common criminal and taken out of the mall.
Summer had been waiting faithfully in the hallway
near the security office, and when she saw me being
escorted away by the police, she went off.

"Where are you taking her? Wait!" Summer said
loudly as she followed the officers.

"Move out of the way, young lady, before we arrest
you along with your friend," the cop warned.

Summer stepped off, but I heard her yell, "Tara, I'll
contact your parents."

Embarrassed and afraid, I did not reply, I just
dropped my head and walked out. It was the first time
I had ever been in trouble, and I only had one person
to blame—Mya.